THE VENOM OF IRON EYES

The notorious gang led by Peg Leg Grimes is headed to the remote and peaceful town of Cooperville to rob the bank of its recently obtained hoard of golden eagles. But unknown to the gang, the bounty hunter Iron Eyes is in town to collect a reward. When the bank explodes into match-wood, Iron Eyes vows to get the money, and the outlaws — for Grimes has made one mistake: he has stolen Iron Eyes' prized Palomino stallion to make his escape . . .

RORY BLACK

THE VENOM OF IRON EYES

Complete and Unabridged

LINFORD
Leicester

First published in Great Britain in 2012 by
Robert Hale Limited
London

First Linford Edition
published 2014
by arrangement with
Robert Hale Limited
London

A catalogue record for this book is available
from the British Library.

ISBN 978–1–4448–1812–3

Published by
F. A. Thorpe (Publishing)
Anstey, Leicestershire

Set by Words & Graphics Ltd.
Anstey, Leicestershire
Printed and bound in Great Britain by
T. J. International Ltd., Padstow, Cornwall

This book is printed on acid-free paper

*Dedicated to the memory
of Laura Bessie Wall.*

Prologue

The rifle shots cut up into the red sky as the small figure on the shotgun guard's seat next to the stagecoach driver heralded their approach. The fiery embers of a setting sun made everything look as though the world was ablaze. Dust rose up like twisters from the hoofs and wheels of the thundering vehicle as it ploughed through everything in its path to reach its goal. The folks of Cooperville had seen many things cross their boundaries over the years but nothing had prepared any of them for the terrifying sight which greeted their weary eyes a few moments after sunset.

It was not the stagecoach drawn by six snorting horses which chilled them into horrified disbelief. Nor was it the smaller figure firing the repeating rifle. It was the barely human form perched high in the driver's box that froze their souls.

The skeletally-featured creature with reins in one hand and a sixteen-foot-long bullwhip in the other hardly appeared human at all. He seemed to be more akin to a Gothic monster from ancient tales brought from distant countries far across the vast expanse of ocean which separated an old land from a new one.

Stunned people ran off the streets in fear of what they were witnessing. No artist had ever managed to paint a picture proclaiming the horrors of Hell and damnation quite as vivid as this sight before their stunned eyes.

The scars of years of brutal conflict were carved into his thin face for all to see. Every detail was highlighted by the cruel, unforgiving blood-coloured sky. A mane of matted hair bounced on his shoulders like the wings of some monstrous bird of prey in search of its next victim.

The stagecoach ploughed through

the outskirts of the settlement.

Every watcher's heart beat faster.

Who was this? What was this?

Rippling scarlet flames stretched out across the heavens as the sun's last dying rays fought their nightly duel with the inevitable coming of darkness. The devil himself could not have created such a hideous apparition as that which met the eyes of the stunned onlookers.

The driver whipped the shoulders of the six charging horses with rods of fire as the crimson light danced off his reins and bullwhip.

Vainly attempting to escape their merciless master the terrified team of horses thundered through the streets, dragging their heavy burden whilst the ear-splitting cracking of the whip rang out above their heads. Tied to the tailgate a large palomino stallion and a small burro had managed to keep pace throughout the relentless journey.

Again the rifle blasted lead up into the air.

An acrid aroma trailed the stagecoach

as it forged on at breakneck speed through the town's meandering streets. It was the scent of death. For, unknown to all those who watched the diabolical sight, the interior of the stagecoach contained a rotting cargo of dead outlaws. A journey of a hundred miles across a baking-hot desert had not been kind to the dead.

The smell was proof of that.

Clouds of dust kicked up off wheel rims as the driver hauled his reins to one side and managed to steer the team around an acute corner before lashing his reins across their backs and getting them back into full flight. The crimson sky reflected off every glass window-pane along the street. A ghastly demonic hue seemed to illuminate the coach and its charging horses as well as the ghostlike creature who was steering it. Somehow the long stagecoach remained on all four wheels as it careered on and on whilst navigating one corner after another.

The springs of the vehicle screamed

out for mercy whilst the team of lathered-up horses kept up the pace demanded of them by the man balancing in the driver's box high above their steaming backs.

None of those who watched the unexpected arrival of the coach would ever forget the sight, which froze their souls. Nothing like this had ever happened in Cooperville before. Until now the Devil had given them a wide berth.

A bone-chilling yell came from the whip-wielding driver as he spun and then jerked at the whip. The cracking sound resembled a six-shooter being fired.

It drew every wide-open eye.

A million questions flashed through the alarmed minds of those who looked on at the unbelievable sight. Had Satan somehow managed to find a way out of the bowels of Hell? Had he finally come to claim their heartless souls?

The scores of coal-tar lanterns had all been lit throughout Cooperville. A

5

fiery avenue was now inviting the strange apparition to venture deeper into the town than anyone really thought wise. But they were all helpless to do anything except stand and watch.

The malodorous stagecoach continued. Halfway along the wide street a large livery stable stood adjacent to a well-lit double-fronted office. Glowing amber lanterns inside and outside the sturdy building lured the uninvited visitor. They beckoned the howling driver as if he were a moth being drawn to their illumination.

A sign protruded away from the overhanging porch directly beneath one of the bright lanterns. It read 'Overland Stagecoach Company' in flaking paintwork.

The menacing figure aimed the spent team at the wooden uprights. The driver sat back down, tossed the whip on to the roof of the coach behind him and gathered the reins up into his bony hands.

He placed the boot of his right leg on

to the brake pole. He leaned back, heaved on the reins and pushed his foot down hard on the brake.

The brakes in their turn shrieked out for mercy.

This time they were heard.

The coach came to an abrupt halt outside the office.

A cloud of dust swamped over the rocking vehicle and the people brave enough to venture towards it. Every eye was on the pair of dust-caked people seated high on the lofty perch.

They were a strange couple by anyone's standards. Even seated the difference in their statures was obvious.

With the stagecoach stationary the stench of death grew stronger as the sickening fumes wafted out from inside the vehicle into the evening air. It was indescribable but neither of the pair who remained on the driver's board appeared to notice. It was as though they were immune to its nauseating odour.

The crowd had become slightly braver as the sky turned to black above

Cooperville. Perhaps they wrongly thought that there was safety in the shadows among which most of them lingered. The sound of the boardwalk creaking under the weight of the approaching sheriff drew the cold bullet-coloured eyes of the man still holding the reins in his bony hands. He could see the gleaming star pinned to the black vest that barely managed to straddle the lawman's girth. As the sheriff drew closer his expression changed as his nostrils filled with the stench coming from the coach.

Sheriff Jonas Welch held the tails of his bandanna to his face and continued towards the pair who were staring down at him.

'What in tarnation is that god-awful stink?' Welch managed to ask as he fought to keep his dinner down.

'What stink?' the driver drawled quietly.

Welch feverishly waved his free hand at the coach. 'That one. What ya got in there? Skunks?'

'Dead 'uns,' the low, whispering voice

of the driver replied as he wrapped the reins around the brake pole and secured them as tightly as he could contrive. 'Ain't ya ever got a noseful of dead 'uns before, Sheriff?'

The door of the stage depot abruptly opened and a bald man wearing a black visor stepped out. The man raised both hands to his face and recoiled as he too inhaled on the sickly stench. He looked at the heavily damaged coach before him and then up at the pair of figures covered in the dust of a hundred miles.

'That's my missing stagecoach,' he said through the gaps in his fingers. 'Did you do this?'

The driver glanced down on him. 'We brung it back for ya.'

'Look at the damage to it,' the depot man said. 'What's that stink? What have you got inside there?'

'Dead 'uns,' the driver drawled.

'Rotting bodies? Oh, sweet Lord,' the depot man yelped like a puppy that had just got its tail caught in a door. 'You've filled one of our coaches with dead people? The interior of the coach is ruined. The finest leathers, silks and cottons are used to meet our customers' every comfort or whim.'

Suddenly a long, thin arm reached down, grabbed hold of the complaining depot man by the throat and lifted him up until he was balanced on his toes. Then the barrel of a long Navy Colt came poking down into the face of the distraught man. The driver cocked its hammer.

For what seemed to be the longest of times nothing happened as the gun barrel slid across the sweating brow of the terrified man.

Then the driver spat.

The spittle hit the depot man dead between his eyes and ran down his nose.

The driver then released his grip and allowed the now silent depot man to stagger towards the sheriff.

'S-Sheriff?' the croaking voice gasped.

Welch shrugged. 'I thought he was gonna blow ya head off there, Elmer.'

'Ain't ya gonna do nothing?'

'I'm biding my time, son. Biding my time,' the lawman huffed.

The skeletal thumb allowed the gun hammer to ease itself back down against the body of the Navy Colt. The deadly gun was then pushed into the man's pants belt. Welch noticed that there was an identical weapon already lingering against the flesh of the stagecoach driver, behind a belt buckle.

'Stay calm, everyone,' the sheriff gruffed before waving a finger at the pair sitting high up. 'And don't go throttling nobody else. Ya hear? If there's any throttling to do I'll do it.'

'I hear.' The rasping voice came from the driver. 'He's lucky I didn't put me a bullet where I put that spit, Sheriff. He's lucky I don't like wasting lead on worthless critters like him.'

The depot man looked outraged. 'Worthless, am I?'

'Ya ain't got bounty on ya, have ya?' The question came through a cloud of falling dust as the bony fingers ran

11

through the mane of long hair. 'If ya have I'll kill you.'

'What?' The man began to run. He headed through the onlooking crowd to the telegraph office. 'J. Finnigan Morely will hear about this.'

'Who in tarnation is J. Finnigan . . . ?'

'The president of the Overland Stage Company,' Welch answered. The lawman tried to keep calm as he pushed the bandanna into his face but he could still smell the sickening aroma of death. He wanted to throw up but he knew that never made a favourable imprssion on voters in an election year. He cleared his throat and tried to sound as though he were in control. 'I figured it was dead folks you had in there but what in blue thunder have you brought them to Cooperville for?'

'Bounty,' the driver answered in a rasping tone.

'What?' Welch could not stop his eyebrows disappearing under the band of his hat.

'Got me a whole heap of wanted

vermin inside this crate.' The driver sighed as he pulled a twisted cigar from his deep trail-coat pocket and rammed it between his teeth. 'I come to claim the reward money on these ornery varmints.'

'Why here?' Welch tried to venture nearer but the aroma kept him back, close to the stagecoach depot door.

'Ya gotta bank, ain't you?' This time it was not the driver who spoke but the creature seated next to him, covered in a couple of inches of dust. So much dust that it was impossible to make out any detail concerning the smaller person.

Welch lowered his bandanna briefly before returning it to his face. The interlude was long enough for him to pose a question.

'Are you a gal?' he asked.

There was a united gasp from the gathering crowd as they too suddenly realized that the voice had sounded far higher-pitched than most men's.

Sheriff Welch screwed up his eyes but could not make anything out clearly of either of the two figures. 'I asked you a question. Are you a gal?'

'What of it?' the smaller figure snapped before hauling a Winchester up from between her legs and cranking its mechanism into action. The barrel was trained down on the fat-chested lawman. 'Ain't no law bin broken. What if I am a gal? I can outshoot any man I ever come across.'

The bony hand of the man sitting on the driver's seat slowly rose and pushed the barrel of the repeating rifle down. The hand then reached out to the lantern closest to the top of the stagecoach and raised its glass bowl. The driver leaned slightly across the distance between the vehicle and the building. With the cigar gripped in his teeth he allowed the black weed to touch the wick of the coal-tar lantern. He then sucked in the smoke and returned back to his original position.

'Take it easy. Don't go killing no lawman, Squirrel. Ain't no profit in it.'

Smoke encircled the head of the lean

man as he stared down at Welch once again. This time even the dust could not conceal the resolve there was in him.

'Listen up, Sheriff. I'm a bounty hunter and these dead 'uns are all wanted dead or alive,' the whispering voice announced through a cloud of smoke. 'I intend collecting.'

'Why'd you kill 'em?' the sheriff asked coyly.

'They was trying to kill me.'

'Us,' the female corrected. 'They was trying to kill us. And another thing: we're both bounty hunters.'

The head of the bounty hunter swung around. 'What? You ain't no bounty hunter, Squirrel. Ya just a little gal that I ain't bin able to shake off for the longest while.'

Squirrel Sally Cooke gave a loud grunt, grabbed the cigar from his mouth and sucked in a lung full of its toxic smoke before folding her arms around the Winchester. 'I saved ya life, didn't I? How many times? Two, three, or was it four?'

'Ya also shot me,' the driver added quietly.

'That's a nice thing to say to ya betrothed.' Squirrel snorted. Smoke trailed from her nostrils. 'You just can't let it drop, can ya? A gal is allowed to shoot her betrothed.'

'What?'

Welch was almost speechless. Almost but not quite. 'How'd I know if these dead folks were wanted or not?' he demanded. 'For all I know you might have just killed them and thought about trying ya luck in Cooperville.'

The long lean figure stood in the driver's box, grabbed the brake pole and swung his leg over until his boot connected with the stagecoach wheel. He then dropped down to the board-walk outside the depot. It was like watching water trickle down a wall. Fluid and with no visible signs of effort.

'Ya doubting my word?'

The sheriff felt nervous. He tried to keep eye contact with the taller man but it was hopeless. There was no amount of dust that could hide the hideous scar-covered face from even the poorest eyesight. Few men could look into those eyes for long without seeing their own death riding up towards them.

'N . . . no. I'm not doubting you, stranger,' Welch stammered.

'Sure sounded like ya was,' Squirrel Sally piped up from her high perch above them. 'That fat old man is calling you a liar, Iron Eyes.'

Another gasp went around the crowd of onlookers.

'W . . . what did she just call you, stranger?' Welch gulped hard but there was no spittle in his tumble-weed-dry throat.

'My name.'

'Ya ought to be mighty feared, Sheriff.' Squirrel Sally grinned as she savoured the smoke of her cigar.

The sheriff looked the man before him up and down. Every story he had ever heard of the creature known as Iron Eyes seemed to be true. The only difference was that the bounty hunter looked even uglier than those tales implied.

'You mean that you are Iron Eyes?' The sheriff felt a cold dampness in his pants front. 'The real Iron Eyes?'

The lantern-light danced in the cold unblinking eyes of the bounty hunter as he opened the door of the stagecoach beside him. A few of the decomposing corpses slid out on to the boardwalk. A slurry of human putrefaction trailed their liquifying bodies. The lean man looked back into the terrified face of the sheriff, then pulled a handful of Wanted posters from his coat pocket and offered them to Welch.

The shaking hands of the sheriff accepted the crumpled posters.

'Yep,' the bounty hunter drawled. 'I am Iron Eyes.'

1

The sound of a coyote filled the air as the dust rose off the hoofs of the small band of deadly riders. The sky had blackened along the high rim above the fast-moving river as the gang of hardened outlaws approached the small village a half-mile below their high vantage point. None of the horsemen knew the name of the settlement of whitewashed adobes. It did not matter to them for they had other things preying on their minds.

This was just a brief interlude along the trail for them. A place for their horses to be grained and watered whilst they fuelled their bellies with vittles and hard liquor.

This was the last stop before they continued on their way to the prosperous yet still remote Cooperville. Four of the band of wanted men were new to this region and it had forced their leader Revis 'Peg Leg' Grimes to hire an outlaw familiar with this strange terrain. Against the wishes of his three followers Grimes had hired a tiny white-whiskered man known as Stogey Swift to guide them to their chosen destination. Belying his outward appearance Swift was quite as deadly as any of them.

So far Swift had proved to be even better than his reputation had boasted, and he had managed to steer them within five miles of Cooperville without their encountering another living soul along the way. Yet it was not getting to Cooperville that was important to the gang, it was managing to escape unscathed.

Steam rose up towards the new moon from the five riders as well as their bone-weary mounts as they steered down through giant boulders towards the river and the beckoning village.

The aroma of chilli cooking on a fiery range filled the nostrils of the deadly gunmen as they trailed Swift ever lower into the canyon.

Behind Swift the one-legged Grimes gripped his reins tightly in his gloved hands whilst he surveyed everything that lay about them. Just behind the tail of Grimes's grey gelding Laredo Cole chewed on the last of his tobacco. Cole was as deadly as they came in these or any other parts. A man who had long run out of room on his gun grips to add any more notches. His only weakness was a bitter, unbalanced hatred of Mexicans and normally he would never have ventured this far south. As he chewed on his tobacco and spat he silently cursed.

Directly behind Cole came the most valuable man of the entire gang. By appearance Boston Brown looked more like a riverboat gambler than anything else most Westerners had ever set eyes upon but, as with most things, the truth was very different.

Brown was an expert with explosives.

Any kind of explosives.

Years earlier he had been tagged as

Dynamite Brown and the name described him and his unusual skill perfectly.

Those who'd known him in his prime would tell of how he could handle any explosive known to man. He was fearless. Brown had become a legend as a man who could make dynamite do exactly what he wanted it to do. In his prime he had aided some of the most notorious bank robbers to achieve their goals for a fifty-per-cent cut of the profits. Gangs had been more than willing to pay his price.

But Boston Brown was no longer in his prime.

He still had the ability to destroy anything he wished to destroy with the minimum of effort, but his health and his judgement had started to go sour.

Those who knew him blamed his liking for dance-hall whores for his recent downfall. Some said he had lung fever. Whatever the truth was, it had soured his once unparalleled genius with the lethal high explosives. Although he was still capable of doing his job, there was a tendency for him to make mistakes. And men who juggle with dynamite for a living should never make even the smallest of mistakes.

The last of the riders eating the dust of the four horsemen ahead of his pinto was aged somewhere in his early twenties. But, for all his youth, he was as experienced as any of the others. A brutal knife-scar carved his otherwise young-looking face in half from temple to chin. His nose had mended badly and was twisted where the flesh of his face had pulled it in two separate directions years earlier.

Winston Parsons rode high in his stirrups. Like Grimes, his eyes never stopped searching for potential trouble. It was his job to kill anything that looked remotely as if it might give them grief. Most times he just killed because it was the easiest option.

Even before the five horses had reached level ground a few dogs began to herald their arrival by barking for all they were worth. The starlight danced across the river and blinded the few people who had ventured from their small white buildings to see who or what was headed their way.

This was a place where they were well used to strangers and none of the onlookers seemed overly concerned at the sight of the five heavily armed riders.

The river was shallow at the foot of the canyon and the outlaws had no problem steering their mounts straight through its ice-cold flow.

'What they call this place?' Grimes enquired loudly.

'This little town is known as Red Pepper, Grimes,' Stogey Swift replied. 'Folks come from all around to eat the grub they makes here. Mighty fine eating.'

Grimes glared at the few faces he could see watching their approach.

Angrily Laredo Cole drove his spurs into his horse and drew level with the one-legged rider. He leaned across to Grimes. His voice was pitched to find the ears of Grimes and not the man who had led them here.

'This is a damn Mex town, Peg Leg.' He spat. 'I hates me Mex critters.'

Grimes nodded slowly. 'I know that, but there are an awful lot of the varmints around these parts.'

'Why'd we come this far south?' Cole questioned.

'We come this far south coz this is where Cooperville is, Laredo,' Grimes answered. 'And if my information is right, that bank has had its safe swollen with a lotta fresh-minted gold coin.'

Laredo Cole fumed. 'Can ya smell 'em? Can ya? They ain't no better than animals. I don't cotton to their breed. They should all be killed. Hear me?'

'I hear ya.' Grimes nodded. 'But we gotta let the nags rest up. We'll need them fresh if'n we're gonna make a clean getaway from that town.'

'Ya knows I hates Mexicans, Peg Leg,' Cole repeated with a gush of venom most men never display. 'You know what they done to my kin? I vowed I'd kill me every last one of them.'

Faster than the deadly Cole had imagined possible, a gloved hand grabbed hold of his bandanna, twisted it tight and then dragged the outlaw towards him. Cole had to cling to his saddle horn just to remain astride his horse.

'No killing,' Grimes growled in a low tone. 'Not until we reach Cooperville do ya even touch them hoglegs of yours. Do ya savvy, Laredo? Do ya?'

Brown tobacco spittle dribbled from the mouth of the younger outlaw. The eyes of the leader of the gang burned through the eerie half-light into Cole's.

Laredo Cole gave a blinking nod. 'Yep.'

Grimes released his grip, then slapped his reins across the shoulders of his mount. It cantered through the water until he was level with Swift.

'They got any fresh horses in this Red Pepper, Stogey?'

'I sure doubt it, Grimes,' Swift replied, rubbing his neck thoughtfully. 'These folks are mostly farmers. They might have a few milk cows out back of one of these adobes but I never seen any horseflesh around here.'

Grimes bit his lip as their five horses reached dry land once more. He eased back on his reins and slowed his grey to a walk.

'Damn,' he muttered. 'I was counting on horses. Fresh horses.'

Swift looked at the troubled expression on the gang leader's face. It was the first time he had seen any hint of concern.

'Ya looks a tad worried.'

'I was hoping these folks might have spare horses we could exchange after we head on back here after we rob that juicy bank over at Cooperville,' Grimes explained as they all moved towards the beaded curtain outside the cantina. A fragrant aroma of cooking engulfed them. 'I figured that a posse would have themselves an awful hard time keeping up with us from here if we had fresh horses and they didn't. Yep. I figured they'd more than likely quit once they trailed us to here.'

Swift gave a nod. 'I see ya point, Grimes.'

The three men behind the two older horsemen dismounted and tethered their reins to a long rickety hitching rail set to the side of the adobe.

Thoughtfully Swift lifted his tiny frame up and slid down to the ground. He looped his reins over the head of the sweating horse. 'We could rustle us up some extra nags in Cooperville.'

Grimes nodded. 'Reckon so.'

Swift watched the one-legged rider ease himself down to the ground and then drag a long crutch from out of the saddle's rifle scabbard. With the crutch under his armpit and his carved stump of a right leg Grimes looked more like a pirate than a bank robber.

'How'd ya lose that leg, Grimes?'

Snorting angrily Grimes rammed his reins into the hands of the inquisitive man and spat on the ground. He looked hard into Swift's face, then pushed his way through the beaded draped curtains and entered the cantina.

Brown walked slowly to Swift and tutted. 'Never ask him how he lost that leg, Swift.'

'Why not?'

'You want to live a little longer, don't you?'

The four men entered the cantina and then found where the grim-faced Grimes was seated. They dragged chairs and stools from around the interior of the place and one by one sat down around the same table.

'Smells good,' Parsons noted.

'Stinking Mexican filth,' Cole snapped. 'Fit only for dogs.'

A busty female smiled as she approached the table. Sweat beads danced on her face and dripped down into her ample cleavage.

'You like food, *amigos*?' she asked them.

Four men nodded. Cole remained snarling.

'Just four bowls of ya best chilli, sweetheart.' Swift grinned before pointing at Cole. 'Laredo ain't got no appetite.'

She moved closer to the grouchy outlaw and touched his face with her soft left hand. 'You no want food, handsome one?'

Cole jerked his head back. 'Git going, lady.'

'Laredo!' Grimes raised his voice but it did not seem to find the ears of his top gun.

'Git going or I'll kill ya,' Cole spat. His spittle hit her apron and ran down its length until it fell to the tiled floor.

She seemed confused and turned away. Then, for some reason known only to himself, Cole drew one of his guns and cocked its hammer.

Before any of the others could do anything to prevent him Cole squeezed the trigger. The deafening white flash sent the bullet into her back. Blood exploded from her chest as she turned with startled eyes and stared at the man who had just ended her life. She fell forward and crashed on to the floor. A pool of blood rippled out from her lifeless body.

'Ya mindless animal.' Grimes lifted his crutch and swung it hard. Its ferruled end caught Cole across the side of his head and sent him cartwheeling off his chair. The outlaw landed next to his victim.

Parsons jumped to his feet and tried to brush the gore from his clothing and face. 'Why'd he do that? Why'd Laredo do it?'

'Because he's loco,' Dynamite Brown said with a sigh.

Grimes managed to stand up. He could hear the sound of the other people in the small settlement heading to the cantina. A grim expression carved across his face as he rested his knuckles on the table.

'How many folks in Red Pepper, Stogey?' he whispered to Swift.

'Twenty or thirty I guess,' Swift answered. 'Why?'

Grimes ran a hand over his face. 'Coz we're gonna have to kill every last one of 'em. That's why.'

Swift jumped to his feet. 'Why?'

Grimes pointed his finger at the body of the female. 'That's why. If we don't kill 'em we'll all pay with our necks.'

Cole groaned and then struggled up off the floor. Blood dripped from him. It was his victim's blood. For a few brief seconds he stared at the gun in his hand, then his eyes lifted until they were burning into Grimes.

'I ought to kill ya for that, Peg Leg,' he said, rubbing the side of his bruised head.

Grimes inhaled deeply. 'Ya want to kill something, boy? Then go out there and kill as many Mexicans as you can damn well find.'

'Yeah?' Cole began to smile.

'Yeah,' Grimes sighed.

A twisted grin curled across the face of the outlaw. He drew his other six-shooter. The outlaw marched through the blood and left a trail of crimson boot-prints in his wake. He pushed the beaded curtain apart and gave out a hideous whooping sound.

Then the shooting started. Red

Pepper resounded to the deafening gunfire. Each shot was accompanied by a scream and a chilling laugh from Laredo Cole.

Grimes eased himself back down on to his chair and pulled a cigar from his coat pocket. He leaned towards the candle set in the centre of the table. He sucked in smoke and glanced at the confused Parsons.

'Ya want to go help Laredo, Winston?' he asked.

The normally ruthless gunhand screwed up his eyes. 'Reckon not, Peg Leg. This kinda killing don't sit well in my craw.'

Brown raised a hand to his mouth and coughed as more and more shots rang out. 'That's because it ain't normal killing, boy. It's nothing but slaughter.'

Grimes exhaled a long line of smoke. 'One day that critter will more than likely turn them hoglegs on us.'

'I still don't understand why he done that,' Parsons said. He stared at the body of the female. 'He had no call to do that.'

Before the beaded curtain had stopped moving Red Pepper fell into a deathly silence. Only the laughter of Laredo Cole could be heard by those inside the cantina as the outlaw searched for more helpless victims.

2

The stench of the decomposing bodies, which had been taken to the funeral parlour, lingered in Cooperville. It had taken the promise of a bottle of whiskey each before the sheriff had been able to recruit anyone to volunteer to undertake the sickening chore. Yet less than an hour after the unexpected arrival of the stagecoach things in Cooperville were starting to get back to normal.

The smell of carbolic soapy water now filled the nostrils of those who walked and rode up and down the lantern-lit streets as frantic store-owners desperately attempted to wash the scent of death away from their businesses.

In all the confusion and activity few noticed the tall man in the long battle-scarred trail coat as he led his dust-caked stallion in search of a place where it might be fed and watered before the long hours of night.

He was like a phantom drifting between the cascading lantern-light and the multitude of black shadows which filled the wide streets. The dishevelled Iron Eyes led his exhausted palomino towards another, far larger, livery stable set well away from the one belonging to the Overland Stagecoach Company. Iron Eyes knew that he and his mount would not be welcome at the company's stable after the short but volatile encounter with the depot manager.

Then, just past a large tree growing close to a street corner, the keen eyes of the hunter of men noticed the very thing he had been searching for. At the very end of a long street that wound to the limits of Cooperville, loomed a large, high building. The weathered construction looked as though it had been put up hastily. Gaps along its façade allowed the glowing light of the blacksmith's forge to shine out into the otherwise dimly lit thoroughfare.

Red sparks greeted the tall bounty hunter as he entered the livery stable. Iron Eyes inhaled the familiar odour only found where many horses were stalled.

'Anybody here?' Iron Eyes called out as he held on to the reins of his magnificent horse.

In the darkest recess of the huge interior, where only darkness dwelled, another glow, not unlike that of the forge to his left, drew Iron Eyes's attention. His eyes darted and squinted hard. His flared nostrils then caught the smell of tobacco.

'Ya must be enjoying that pipe, *amigo*,' Iron Eyes ventured.

'I am,' a gruff voice agreed. The glowing pipe started to come closer.

The bounty hunter turned his lean frame and stared at the man who suddenly came into view. He was a man built of muscle and bone. A man who looked as though he had the strength to carry a horse on his shoulders should the desire come to him.

'Damn,' Iron Eyes said. 'You sure are a mighty big man and no mistake.'

The man stopped beside Iron Eyes. He was of the same height but that was where any similarity between them ended. His attention drifted from the thin figure to the dusty horse standing behind its master. No amount of dust could conceal the quality of the horse from knowing eyes.

'That sure is one hell of a fine horse ya got there.'

Iron Eyes briefly cast his attention upon his horse. 'Under that dust there happens to be a palomino.'

The man pocketed his pipe, stepped forward and ran a muscular hand down the nose of the horse. His sweat removed the dust to reveal its white blaze. 'Damn. Never seen me a palomino before. Heard about the critters but I never seen one. Where ya get such a nag in these parts?'

'South of the border,' Iron Eyes drawled. He found a cigar in his pocket and placed it between his teeth. 'He used to belong to a *vaquero*.'

A sly grin crept across the features of the blacksmith. 'Ya kill the bastard for this horse?'

'Yep.' Iron Eyes ran a thumbnail across a match and cupped the flame in his bony hands. He sucked in the smoke. 'He was trying to kill me first, though.'

The blacksmith took the reins from the bounty hunter and allowed the horse to walk around him. 'This ain't like no horse I ever seen and I sure seen me a whole lot of horses. Fine. Mighty fine.'

'I want him washed down, watered and fed,' the bounty hunter said. He savoured the smoke that drifted through his teeth with every word.

'It'd be a damn pleasure, stranger.' The large man sighed. 'I can't wait to see what he looks like without this blanket of dust he's covered in.'

Iron Eyes glanced around the interior of the stable. There were forty stalls and half of them were filled with horses. He then pushed a thumb and finger into his deep coat pocket and pulled out a couple of silver dollars. He handed them to the man who was drooling over the handsome stallion.

'Make sure he has himself a wide stall,' the bounty hunter said. He exhaled more smoke between his teeth. 'He likes to lie down.'

'Ya staying in town long, stranger?' The blacksmith led the stallion into the centre of the livery and wrapped the reins around an upright which stretched up to a sturdy hayloft.

'As long as it takes for the bank to pay me what I'm owed.'

'You the bounty hunter?' the black-smith asked, without making eye contact. 'You the *hombre* they call Iron Eyes?'

'Yep.' Iron Eyes moved toward the nearer of the tall doors and rested a thin hand upon its weathered surface. He stared down the length of the brightly illuminated street. 'Well, ya know my handle. What they call you?'

'They call me Slim,' came the

unexpected reply.

The bounty hunter did not say a word. His expression said it all as he looked at the huge man.

The blacksmith shrugged. 'I was kinda puny when I started work here as a boy. The name sort of stuck.'

Iron Eyes gave a slow nod. 'Sure ain't gonna be hard to remember.'

Slim lit a lantern nailed to the upright. Its light swept over the large horse beside him. He then went to a trough set inside the livery and pushed a bucket through the water. 'I'll wash this horse down right now. Make him feel real fresh before I feed him.'

A groan came from Iron Eyes. The blacksmith turned and watched as the thin man straightened up.

'What's wrong?' Slim asked.

'Ya got a side door out of this place, Slim?' Iron Eyes asked, tossing his cigar away.

'You look like someone who just seen himself a ghost.'

Suddenly Iron Eyes heard his name

being called out at him from halfway down the street. He hunched his shoulders and began to shake his head.

'What in tarnation was that bellowing out ya name?' the blacksmith asked curiously. He moved to stand next to the emaciated bounty hunter. He focused on the small dusty figure which was marching towards them. 'Well, at least it ain't a ghost. Hey, is that a gal?'

Iron Eyes looked over his shoulder at Squirrel Sally as she led her burro towards the livery stable.

'Reckon so. Mind you, she's a damn sight better at haunting a varmint than any ghost I ever heard tell about.' Iron Eyes ran his fingers through his mane of hair. 'Is there a back way out of here, Slim?'

Slim pointed at a dark wall. 'There's a door to the corral over yonder. You can escape out thataway, Iron Eyes.'

'Much obliged.' Iron Eyes nodded.

'You look almost scared,' the blacksmith observed as he carried the bucket of water back to the palomino.

'That Squirrel Sally has a way of unnerving a man, Slim.' Iron Eyes said seriously. 'Ain't normal for a little critter like her to be able to do that to a grown man, but she can.'

Slim smiled as the bounty hunter disappeared into the shadows. 'If that don't beat all. The great Iron Eyes running away from a squirrel.'

3

A flash of lightning suddenly forked across the wide dark sky. A few moments later deafening thunder erupted above Cooperville and shook every wooden structure below its primitive fury. As though from nowhere a cold breeze swept across the plains and was channelled through the streets of the remote town. Iron Eyes drew his collar up and marched through the shadows towards the porch light of the distant sheriff's office.

The sound of his spurs was drowned by the whispering wind as the thin emaciated figure crossed the wide main street, going towards his goal. Another rumble made the night air tremble. The bounty hunter glanced upward and gritted his teeth at the sight of further storm clouds gathering.

The familiar smell and sound of a well-patronized saloon caught the attention

44

of the man who feared nothing except the small female of whom, he hoped, he could keep one step ahead.

Adjusting the pair of Navy Colts which jutted out of his pants belt, Iron Eyes stepped up on to the boardwalk and paused outside a drinking hole called High Garter. His narrow eyes darted up and down the long thoroughfare. It seemed as though every other building was either a saloon or gambling hall. He rested both hands on top of the swing doors and surveyed the interior of the saloon. A few dozen men and a handful of bar-room girls in scanty dresses were oblivious to the onlooker. Pipe and cigar smoke floated around the room. He inhaled the smell of stale beer on old sawdust willingly. Iron Eyes glanced to the far wall where a man in a small round hat played a piano which seemed to have fewer white keys than black.

The bounty hunter pushed the door apart, entered and suddenly all sound of enjoyment stopped. Even the piano ceased its tinny noise.

It was something he had grown used to. Men and bar girls tended to drop everything they were doing when they saw the horrific features of the lone bounty hunter. His thin fingers ran through his long black hair to reveal even more brutal scars to those who still dared look in his direction.

His large vicious spurs rang out their deadly warning with each long stride as Iron Eyes made his way slowly towards the long, well-stocked counter. Men and women parted as he made his way across the large interior of the High Garter. Two men with oiled hair and identical waxed handlebar moustaches watched his approach from behind the bar. They continued to frantically polish glasses and tried to remain calm. It was not easy to give the illusion of total unawareness when such a creature was heading straight for you with his unblinking bullet-coloured eyes burning into your very soul.

Iron Eyes stopped by the bar and rested a boot on the brass rail next to a spittoon. He gave a slow nod to the nearer of the bartenders and curled a finger.

'Y-yes, sir?' The croaking stammer came from behind the black moustache. 'What'll it be?'

There was a short pause, then Iron Eyes nodded at an array of different sorts of whiskey bottles standing just in front of a six-foot-long mirror behind the bartender's back.

'Whiskey,' Iron Eyes said in a low drawl. 'The best ya got.'

The terrified man swallowed hard, plucked one of the bottles from the shelf and showed it to the bounty hunter. 'This good enough, sir?'

Again the tall bounty hunter nodded. 'Yep.'

The bartender exhaled and placed the bottle down in front of the man who had managed to bring the entire saloon to a deafening silence simply by coming through the door. He reached out to a pyramid of whiskey glasses carefully stacked on the end of the counter and took one. He placed it over the cork of the bottle.

'That'll be . . . '

Iron Eyes did not wait to hear the cost of his purchase. He placed a golden eagle down and flicked it across the wet counter to the man.

'Drinks for everyone,' Iron Eyes hissed like a rattler before picking up his purchase and making his way to a recently vacated table.

One of the bravest of the bar-room girls moved away from the crowd and stepped in front of the monstrous-looking bounty hunter. She pressed her body against his and then shuddered when the cold steel of his guns touched the top of her swollen breasts as they fought to remain inside her tight dress.

'You want to come upstairs?' she asked.

'Why?' Iron Eyes asked.

Her fingers peeled the dress down off her white-powdered bosoms to reveal her large apple-coloured nipples. 'This is why, stranger. You like them? You wanna see more?'

Iron Eyes brushed her aside. 'Nope. I got me a pair of teats myself. Ain't never wanted to see anyone else's. Ain't no profit in it.'

'Drinks are on the stranger,' the bartender called out after he had bitten the golden coin. 'Come and get 'em.'

The girl joined the crowd and rushed to the bar to get the free drinks. The tall bounty hunter eased himself around the table and lowered himself on to a chair with its back against the wall. He leaned back, removed the thimble-sized glass and placed it to the side of the bottle. Without saying a word the bounty hunter looked at the piano player and nodded.

The man started to play again.

Still watching every man and woman in the saloon Iron Eyes raised the bottle to his mouth and gripped its cork with his sharp teeth. He pulled it free, then spat it out across the room.

The bounty hunter took a long swallow from the neck of the bottle and allowed the fiery whiskey to burn a trail down to his innards. It tasted good.

Then, directly across from where Iron Eyes was sitting, he saw a man with a wide-brimmed sombrero pulled down over his face suddenly rise from his chair. The man pushed his coat tails over his pair of holstered gun grips. The man then kicked the table aside and stepped out into the centre of the room.

'Reckon ya think ya can buy any damn thing ya likes.' The voice was loud and known to the bounty hunter even if he could not see the face below the hat brim. 'I ain't taking no free drink from a stinking back-shooting bounty hunter, Iron Eyes. Ya hear me? I'd rather drink horse water.'

Iron Eyes lowered the bottle until it rested on the table top. He then sat forward.

'Texas Dan McGraw.' The bounty hunter said the name as if he were sucking poison. 'I thought you was dead and buried.'

McGraw raised a long arm and pointed a shaking finger at the seated bounty hunter. 'I know ya think that ya got some kinda special killing powers, but I'm here to tell ya that ya wrong, boy.'

Iron Eyes knew that this was going to be a hard argument to win by the sound of the drunken rage in McGraw's voice.

'Is this about me killing ya brother, Texas Dan?' Iron Eyes asked. Calmly he placed a cigar between his teeth, then struck a match with his thumbnail. He inhaled the smoke and tossed the match away. 'That was just business.'

With his arm shaking as he kept pointing an accusing finger at the bounty hunter, McGraw tilted his head back to reveal his mutilated face. A face without a nose.

'No it ain't. I don't give me a damn about ya killing old Rufas, Iron Eyes. This is because ya shot my damned nose off in Waco. Remember?'

'Oh.' Iron Eyes slowly rose until he was standing. 'I thought ya had gotten a tad ornery about me killing old Rufe.'

McGraw pointed at his face. 'Look at

me, ya bastard. I ain't got me a nose coz ya shot it off. That weren't a nice thing to do.'

A wry smile crossed the scarred features of the bounty hunter as he flexed his fingers and sucked in more smoke. 'If'n you ask me I think ya look better.'

People were now pressed up against walls on all sides of the saloon praying that when the shooting started there would be no stray bullets flying about.

McGraw took a step. 'What? Ya figure I looks better without a nose, Iron Eyes? Are ya loco?'

'Maybe.' The bounty hunter shrugged. 'But ya gotta admit that it was a real big ugly nose after all. I done ya a favour shooting it off.'

An indignant McGraw staggered closer.

'It weren't as big as Rufas's nose,' McGraw yelled out. 'Did ya shoot his nose off? Well, did ya?'

'I ain't rightly sure. I just blew his head off his shoulders.' Iron Eyes stepped around the table until there was nothing between himself and the irate Texas Dan. 'Ya want to share some fine whiskey with me?'

Iron Eyes had barely lifted the bottle off the table when McGraw drew one of his Remingtons and fired. The bottle shattered into a million fragments. The bounty hunter shook his head, then tossed the neck of the bottle aside.

'Ya shouldn't have done that, Texas Dan. That bottle had a lot of sipping left in it.'

McGraw returned the smoking weapon back to its holster and gave out a hideous grin. 'I ain't scared of you.'

'I figured that.' Iron Eyes held his hands out at hip level and stared hard at the angry man.

McGraw laughed loudly. 'Ya reckon on trying to outdraw me, boy? No one has ever managed to do that.'

'Tell me, Texas Dan. Are ya wanted dead or alive?' Iron Eyes asked.

'I surely am,' McGraw replied proudly.

'How much ya worth?'

'Two hundred dollars.'

'That's mighty fine.' Iron Eyes hands went for the pair of Navy Colts, dragged them from his belt and fired both in quick succession. As two bullets passed through the tails of his long trail coat Iron Eyes watched as both his own shots hit McGraw dead centre and lifted him off his feet. The man went flying backwards and crashed into the bar counter. Blood trailed down the wooden counter as the wanted man fell lifelessly on to his side. 'Two hundred dollars. Mighty fine pickings. I hate wasting lead on folks that ain't worth a plug nickel.'

Every eye watched as the skeletal hand of the bounty hunter gripped the left boot of the dead man and used it to drag Texas Dan McGraw out of the saloon into the dark street.

Lightning flashed for a few seconds as if the Devil was greeting the tall figure who was dragging the dead outlaw towards the sheriff's office. A heartbeat later Cooperville shook as a thunder-clap sounded.

4

The smell of burning air was something which seldom filled the nostrils of anyone in this remote land. It harked back to an ancient time when creatures were totally at the mercy of the elements. Yet even after thousands of years little had really changed. For no man or beast has ever managed to tame nature into submission. Whatever destructive fury it wished to dish out all living, breathing creatures had little choice but to take. Take it or hide until it had passed over. Yet sometimes there were no hiding places. No safe havens.

There was a brutal storm brewing above the parched land. A storm more vicious than the five horsemen had ever encountered before. The riders who had guided their lathered-up mounts from the blood-splattered adobes of Red Pepper to the high crest of the ridge above the sprawling lantern-lit settlement were helpless to do anything.

Grimes drew rein first and stopped the small caravan of deadly riders as they reached the highest point of the long ridge. Steam from riders and mounts alike drifted from them as the evening air grew colder.

The sky had blackened and unchallenged storm clouds moved eastward, taking with them flashes of lethal lightning whilst soul crippling explosions of thunder grew louder and ever closer. Only men with a job to do would have been foolhardy enough to venture out into this storm.

The five outlaws had to dig their boots deep into their stirrups and hold their horses firmly in check as the animals became aware that the high ground was no place to be when nature unleashed its venomous fury.

There was no cover here for either man or beast. Nothing but flat terrain for as far as the eye could see.

Boston Brown brought his skittish

horse up level to the brooding Grimes as the large rider stared down across the range before them at the town of glowing amber illumination.

'What ya thinking, Peg Leg?' Brown asked, fighting to control his horse.

Grimes cast an eye at Brown. 'Thinking we chose the wrong night to come into this god-forsaken land, Dynamite. I'm also thinking of all that money and gold in that bank safe.'

Brown gave a slow nod and shivered as another roar of deafening thunder rolled across the sky above them.

'Reckon this storm might be a blessing in disguise,' the sickly horseman noted. 'It'll start raining pretty soon and when it does all traces of our hoof tracks will be washed away.'

'You might be right there, Dynamite.'

'On the other hand I don't cotton to riding through this storm once it gets up on its hind legs.' Brown shrugged. 'I've seen what happens to folks when they get hit by lightning and it sure ain't a handsome sight.'

'We've come too far for us not to do what we come to do,' Grimes insisted as all five riders' attention was drawn to a spider's web of white death as it forked off to their left and hit the ground. Sparks exploded and flew up into the blackness. The smell of sulphur drifted over them. 'Damn! That was close.'

'Too close,' Brown added. He stared all around them, vainly searching for a place where they might be safe from the rods of forked lightning which were hitting the ground more frequently. 'The only safe place in these parts is Cooperville.'

Grimes agreed. 'Yeah. If nothing else them buildings oughta give us and our nags a chance of not getting ourselves blown to bits by this storm.'

Brown smiled and patted his saddle-bags set just behind his cantle. 'Ain't you forgetting about what I have in these bags, Peg Leg? I got me enough sticks of dynamite here to blow that town off the map.'

Grimes looked at the others before

staring hard at Brown's pale features. 'I trust you, Dynamite. This storm is another thing. No man can trust a storm that can kill anything it damn well likes for no reason.'

A nervous Swift eased his mount closer to the two horsemen as they talked. 'Since I managed to get you here, what ya want me to do when we gets down there, Peg Leg?'

Grimes gave a snort and stared around them at the dark clouded sky. Brief blinding flashes danced unchecked across the vast expanse of what loomed above them. Few men could have witnessed such growing ferocity without being troubled.

'You stick with Winston, Stogey,' the outlaw leader said firmly. He jerked his reins and started his horse on down the long slope, which led to the awaiting town. 'Just don't get yourself killed or we'll never find our way back out of here.'

Swift gave a bearded grin and spurred his mount. 'I ain't figuring on getting myself killed, Peg Leg.'

Laredo Cole stood in his stirrups and rode between Brown and his one-legged boss as the five riders guided their horses to their destination. The ruthless killer had not stopped smiling since they left Red Pepper. As his horse drew level to the gelded grey he glanced across into the stern face of Grimes.

'And what ya want me to do when we gets to Cooperville, Peg Leg?' he shouted.

A snarl seemed to cover the entire face of the one-legged rider as he glared at the man whose sanity he had started to question. 'Keep them hoglegs holstered until I tell ya different, boy. Ya savvy? We don't need no noisy gunplay until we've managed to fillet that bank safe like a fish.'

'I savvy,' Cole cackled.

The riders continued on down towards the lights of the distant Cooperville. Their pace increased as their fearful mounts tried to outrun the following stormclouds.

5

The huge blacksmith had washed most of the dust from the tall stallion before the tiny figure of Squirrel Sally marched barefoot into the livery stable leading her burro by the rope reins she had fashioned for it days earlier. Slim dropped the sodden cloth into the bucket, turned and then stared down at the female who had managed to cause Iron Eyes to flee ten minutes earlier.

'You must be Squirrel,' Slim said, chortling.

She narrowed her eyes and then cranked the Winchester with expert ease. 'How'd ya know that, ya big old galoot?'

'Ya don't need to prime that carbine on my account, gal.'

She swung the barrel around until it was aimed straight up at the taller Slim. 'Iron Eyes has bin here, ain't he?'

'Yep.' Slim smiled widely.

Her eyes looked all around the lantern-lit interior of the livery before returning to the target she had her trusty rifle aimed at.

'Where'd he go?'

'Ya scared the skinny varmint off, gal.' The blacksmith knew that the smallest puppies always barked the loudest and he was wary of getting his ankles bitten. He cautiously moved to her and studied the small burro before nodding.

She looked at the bounty hunter's horse. It was gleaming as water ran down from its high shoulders to the damp sod floor.

'What ya mean?'

Slim leaned over and stroked the back of the tired burro before glancing into her face. It was covered in more trail dirt than the stallion had been but somewhere beneath all the dust he reckoned that there might be a pretty face hiding.

'Like I said. Ya darn scared the pitiful critter.'

Now it was time for Squirrel to smile.

'He done run off coz he was feared of me?'

'Yep. I never seen a man so feared.' Slim took hold of the rope, led the burro into the centre of the livery, then tied it close to the glowing forge. 'Ya little burro will be warm by here.'

'Iron Eyes is feared of little old me?' She burst out laughing. 'He sure is a strange one, ain't he?'

'Them sure is the words I was trying to spit out.'

The female kicked at the dirt floor and then propped the rifle over her shoulder as she moved back to the wide-open doors and stared up at the cruel-looking sky. Lightning was flashing all over the vast heavens. 'I don't cotton to storms.'

Slim walked back to her and rested a mighty hand on the nearer of the tall doors. He squinted hard at the unsettling sky, then plucked the pipe from his pocket and put it in his mouth. 'They say that one day the whole world will come to an end after one real big storm.'

'Ya got any cigars?' she asked.

The blacksmith looked down at her. 'Gals ain't meant to smoke.'

'Who says?' Squirrel looked angered. She moved closer to the man who was beginning to know why Iron Eyes was wary of this tiny creature.

He shrugged. 'I dunno. Folks say it all the time.'

'I like smoking and I like chewing tobacco.' She nodded firmly as her finger wagged in front of him. 'Ya got a spare pipe anyplace?'

'Nope,' Slim answered. 'I only got me this old corn cob.'

'Where'd he go?' Squirrel asked angrily, staring out at the street as the first droplets of rain began to fall. 'Where'd that bounty hunter go, fat boy?'

Slim rubbed his neck. 'He looked thirsty. Maybe he went to get himself a few drinks.'

She nodded as if agreeing with the words. 'Yeah. He'll be trying to get himself drunk in case we has to wrestle later. That'll be it. Yep. He's whiskey hunting.'

'You sure are a frisky little thing,' Slim remarked.

She was about to reply when her keen young eyes caught sight of something on the distant ridge as lightning flashed. 'Did you see that?'

The blacksmith moved towards her and stared in the direction in which she was pointing a small finger. 'See what, Squirrel?'

Another bright but brief eruption of lightning flashed across the hill from which the trail led into the town.

'Riders.'

Slim screwed up his eyes. 'I don't see nothing.'

'Riders. Five of them,' she continued. 'And they're headed here fast and fancy.'

The large man turned away. 'Most likely it's just a bunch of cowboys coming into town for a drink, gal.'

Squirrel looked thoughtful. She kept staring at the approaching horsemen. A thunderclap rocked the very foundations of the livery but neither the large

65

man nor the small female seemed to notice.

'Are there any cows out yonder, big man?' Squirrel Sally asked. 'Cowboys needs cows, otherwise they're something else.'

Slim paused and looked over his shoulder at her. 'Ya right, gal. There ain't no ranches or cattle ranges out thataway. Only a whole heap of sand.'

'So whatever they are they sure ain't cowboys.' She spat.

'I'd not lose no sleep over them, Squirrel,' Slim said. 'We never gets no trouble in these parts.'

The small female nodded to herself. 'There's always a first time. Reckon I'd better go find Iron Eyes and tell the critter that there's a bunch of riders headed into town.'

'They're probably just drifters.'

'I don't cotton to drifters,' she snapped.

'Why ya so interested in them, little 'un?' Slim removed the pipe from his mouth, pushed it back into his pocket, then watched her as she kept staring out at the range.

'I got me the right,' Squirrel whispered.

'How come ya don't cotton to drifters, Squirrel?'

There seemed to be tears in her eyes as the lightning once again lit up the front of the livery stable and bathed them both in its white glory. She lowered her head and gripped her rifle in both hands. Her knuckles whitened.

'Coz it was a stinking bunch of drifters that rode into my ranch and killed all my kinfolk a week or so back.'

Squirrel Sally Cooke moved fast across the vast expanse of livery floor to the glowing warm forge. She plucked a parcel she had been using as a makeshift saddle from the back of the burro and shook it loose as, on small bare feet, she returned to the wide-open doors of the stable. The blacksmith watched silently as she pulled on the large black coat and turned up its tailored silk collar.

The coat had been made for a much taller person. A man who buried folks for a living. Its hem touched the ground around her but she seemed to think it was the most fashionable item of clothing ever created.

'Where'd ya get that coat, gal?' Slim asked.

'Iron Eyes give it to me,' she replied. 'After we left the ranch and headed on out after the varmints that killed my kin. It needs taking in but it sure is warm.'

'Where'd he get it from?' the blacksmith enquired. 'Looks like the kinda coat worn by undertaking folks.'

She gave a firm nod and rested the long barrel of the rifle on her shoulder. 'It sure is. Iron Eyes got it from a dead old undertaker who didn't need it no more.'

The large man had no words left. Every answer left him even more confused. Slim sighed and rubbed the sweat from his face with his giant hands. As he lowered his arms he noticed the small female was gone.

Then the rain came down a little harder.

Slim cast a look at the brooding sky as it continued to threaten its wrath on anyone who tried to challenge its supremacy over mere mortals.

He returned to the stallion.

6

The sound of the lifeless body being dragged along the boardwalk drew Jonas Welch from his wash bowl to the office door. Before he could reach out with a wet hand it swung open towards him. A flash of lightning lit up the tall emaciated bounty hunter as he released the grip on the outlaw's leg.

Welch stared in disbelief at the remains of Texas Dan McGraw as Iron Eyes brushed past him and sat down on a chair next to the lawman's desk.

'What's this?'

'Another outlaw,' Iron Eyes replied.

'Will ya stop bringing me dead bodies, boy?' Welch pleaded as he slammed the door shut and moved to the shoulder of the bounty hunter. The sheriff picked up a scrap of paper and a pencil and sighed. 'Now I gotta do all my figuring over. How much is that 'un worth?'

'Two hundred dollars,' Iron Eyes answered. 'Leastways, that's what he said he was worth.'

The sheriff paused and looked at the seated man. 'Ya asked him how much he was worth?'

Rainwater dripped from the long mane of black hair as Iron Eyes nodded. 'Sure enough. Asked him if he was wanted dead or alive as well. Hell, I don't want folks to think I'm a killer.'

The lawman sat down in the chair next to his hideous guest and licked the end of his pencil. 'I spent two hours getting me a tally of that coachful of bodies ya dumped on me, boy. Now I gotta start all over.'

'That's Texas Dan McGraw,' Iron Eyes whispered. 'Ya probably got paper on him somewhere.'

'Why'd ya kill him?' Welch asked.

'He started it.' Iron Eyes sighed. 'I was trying to have me a long drink of whiskey and he recognized me. He got a tad ornery and one thing led to another.'

71

'But ya had time to have a little chat and then ya found out he was wanted dead or alive so ya killed him?'

'That ain't how it was exactly.'

'How was it?'

'He shot my whiskey bottle,' Iron Eyes recalled. 'I got me a little angry when he done that.'

Welch pointed the pencil at the closed office door. 'Who is this Texas Dan?'

'I killed his brother a year or so back.' The bounty hunter gave a cruel smile. 'That was when I shot Dan's nose off his face. He sure had himself a grudge about that, Sheriff.'

'Ya shot his nose off?' The lawman cleared his throat. 'Why didn't ya kill him then and not just mutilate his face, boy?'

Iron Eyes looked the sheriff in the face. 'That would have bin wrong. Dan wasn't wanted dead or alive back then. Hell, I ain't no killer. I only collect on outlaws with paper on them.'

Welch jotted the figures down and

added up the total. 'A tidy sum and no mistake.'

'I ain't too troubled about the tally, old-timer. As long as I got me whiskey and bullet money.' Iron Eyes rose to his feet, moved to the glass panel of the door and stared out at the rain, which was turning the street into a muddy swamp.

Welch raised an eyebrow and stared at the curious figure. 'I thought ya would be in bed with that little gal by now.'

The bounty hunter glanced at the still seated lawman. 'That ain't funny, Sheriff.'

Welch got back to his feet and studied the bounty hunter who seemed to be concerned about something which the lawman could not fathom.

'What's eating at you, boy? Ya get all high-shouldered when I mentions that gal. Why?'

'Why? She worries me,' Iron Eyes admitted. 'That's why.'

Iron Eyes paced back to the sheriff's desk and rested his knuckles on it. 'Got any whiskey?'

Welch pointed at his coffee cup, which was filled with a black tar-like substance he considered to be coffee. 'Do ya honestly think I'd be drinking this rat poison if'n I had me any whiskey in this office, boy?'

There were beads of sweat trailing down Iron Eyes's scarred face. He looked nervous and that confused the older man.

'Why are ya troubled about that little filly, Iron Eyes?'

Iron Eyes shook his head. 'Damned if I rightly know.'

Jonas Welch rubbed his double chins in turn. 'I never seen a grown man so fearful of a female before. How come she worries ya, boy?'

The taller man straightened up to his full impressive height and stared down at the listening law officer. 'It's like this, Sheriff. I rode into her ranch a few days back and she opened up with a rifle and shot a couple of chunks of flesh off my hide.'

Welch felt his eyebrows rise. 'Oh.'

The bounty hunter carried on. 'I had me some trouble with my eyes at the time and was a tad blind. So I didn't know she was a gal. If ya get my drift?'

Welch nodded. 'So she got the drop on ya?'

'Yep.' Iron Eyes also nodded as he recalled how he and Squirrel Sally had first encountered one another. 'Then I played possum. She come up close to finish me off and then I kinda grabbed her legs and brung her down. We wrestled for a while and I got on top of her. She was wriggling like a sidewinder but I managed to get the rifle out of her hands. That's when the trouble started.'

'How do ya mean?' Welch was starting to enjoy the tale.

'Well, I didn't know she was a gal and I sort of got me a real handful of her female bits. Her chest and all.' Iron Eyes swallowed hard. 'That was when I figured she weren't a man. That's when it all got kinda confusing.'

'How do ya mean?'

There was a long painful silence,

then Iron Eyes looked right at the man with the cup to his lips. 'She said we was gonna have to get hitched and the like.'

Sheriff Welch managed not to laugh. 'I don't reckon that's right, boy. Just coz ya had a grope of her feminine parts don't mean ya committed to marriage.'

'She said that's how babies is made.' The bounty hunter sighed, shook his head and stared at the floor. 'I reckon she was lying, but, looking the way I do, I ain't had me a whole lot of truck with females.'

The lawman walked to the window and stared out at the street. He kept the cup as close to his face as possible for fear of angering the thin figure standing by his desk.

'She might actually believe that,' Welch said thoughtfully. 'Not many young gals ever learn anything until their wedding night.'

Iron Eyes looked pitifully across the room at the sheriff. 'I ain't bin able to shake the gal off my tail since then. We had us this run-in with all them outlaws that killed her kinfolks and she did sorta save my bacon a couple of times, but I'm starting to get troubled. Hell, I ain't slept in over a week.'

'How come?'

'Ain't bin possible. If I was to lie down someplace she'd be there next to me doing things.' Iron Eyes rose back up and started to pace around the room. 'I had her hands down my pants all the way here. Kinda unsettling.'

Welch gave out a cough to disguise his choking laughter. 'I thought she looked like the type to be touching folks in private places. Some gals just can't keep their hands off a man.'

'She sure is troubling, Sheriff.' Iron Eyes moved next to the sheriff and peered out into the lantern-lit street. 'I drove that stinking coach a hundred miles without stopping and she had her hands down inside my pants pockets every one of them miles. She was feeling me. You know?'

Welch placed a hand on the wide shoulder. 'I know. My memory serves me well. I ain't had any gal come close to my pants pockets in the longest while but I still recall.'

'Ain't natural.' Iron Eyes swallowed hard and shuddered. 'Now she wants me to get us a room in one of the hotels in town, but I don't like the idea. Next thing ya know I'll be hogtied and taken to a preacher like a lamb to the slaughter.'

'What does she look like under all that dust?'

The bounty hunter blinked. 'Damned if I know. I ain't seen her with a clean face.'

'She might be pretty.'

'So?' Iron Eyes looked up at the wall clock. 'What time does the bank open in the morning? When can I get me my bounty money, Sheriff? I wanna hightail it.'

'The bank don't open until ten.'

'Damn,' Iron Eyes cursed.

'You'll be a mighty wealthy man

when Hogan the banker pays you that reward money. I figure it comes to thousands.' Welch almost sounded envious. Then he looked at the mutilated features of his strange companion and all envy evaporated.

'If I give her half the reward money do ya reckon she might go hunting for another man, Sheriff?' The bounty hunter grabbed hold of the office door handle and turned it. 'I don't cotton to having her on my tail for the rest of my days. I am Iron Eyes. I always ride lonesome.'

'Give it all to her and she'll be swamped by every money-grabbing varmint in Cooperville,' The lawman suggested with a smile.

Iron Eyes pulled the door towards him and stepped out on to the boardwalk. 'I might just do that.'

'Do what?' The voice took both men by surprise. Iron Eyes looked down and stared at the female leaning against the office wall.

'Ya found me, Squirrel.'

'I just followed the blood from that saloon down yonder.'

'I had me a run-in with an old pal.' Iron Eyes aimed a finger at the dead body propped against the porch upright.

'There's riders headed into town,' she blurted out.

'So?'

'How many riders, young lady?' Welch queried.

'Five and they're loaded for bear,' Squirrel answered.

Iron Eyes sighed. 'Probably just drifters, Squirrel.'

Welch was thoughtful. 'Maybe.'

She grabbed Iron Eyes's coat-sleeve and began to walk with him in tow. 'Come on. I found me a real smart hotel down the street a piece. Booked us a room. Told them you'd pay.'

The lawman smiled and watched the tiny female in the long coat leading the thin bounty hunter across the wide street. He then closed the office door.

7

Totally oblivious to the storm which was now directly over Cooperville a sixty-year-old man was feverishly working inside a well-constructed wooden building. Bank owner Barton Hogan had never been the sort of man to burn the midnight oil or do anything which his employees could not handle for him, but the previous three days had been different from any that had gone before.

For the very first time the monthly payroll for the Mason silver mine had been entrusted to the already wealthy banker. At a mere five per cent interest Hogan's Bank had made by far the cheapest tender for the contract to handle the mining company's business.

Three days earlier two hefty metal strongboxes had arrived on the west-bound stagecoach from El Paso. Both boxes were filled with thousands of dollars of fresh-minted golden eagles to be sorted and turned into paper money for transporting to the mine where it would be paid out in wages. But Hogan was not a man to stand by and watch other more hard-working men get paid without doing what all bankers do: try to find a way of milking some of those wages from their rightful recipients before they even were paid.

On every night after the arrival of the strongboxes, as soon as the bank had closed for business and Hogan had sent his two tellers home, the eager banker had been carefully calculating the profit he could make by a little creative bookkeeping.

Hogan had not become rich by accident. Men like him never left anything to chance. Especially when it came to money. Golden eagles had a fluctuating value and fortunes could be made by shrewd men who knew how to wait until the pendulum swung in their favour.

The mining company had entrusted the dealing with the monthly payroll to Hogan's Bank. That was the sort of error many other companies had made over the previous twenty years.

The man turned the brass lamp-wheel and bathed the office in bright light. He licked the tip of his pencil and jotted down his calculations on a scrap of paper. What he was doing was not meant to be emblazoned in ink upon an official ledger page. That was where many of his breed had gone wrong in the past. The evidence of what he was doing was for his eyes alone.

There would be no official records to be used against him should anyone have the wits to work out that they had been expertly fleeced.

A wry smile crossed his face as he tucked the pencil behind his ear and stared at the open safe. The six-foot-high safe was filled from the bottom shelf to the top with the gleaming golden coins. They were now his to resell whenever the mood took him.

Hogan's eyes drifted to the long table beside the safe. He had made twenty piles of carefully counted bank notes in exchange for the valuable coins.

If the miners thought they were going to be paid as usual in gold coin they were going to be sadly mistaken. Hogan had made sure the contract did not specify what the payroll would consist of. As long as it was legal tender there could be no objections.

Five per cent was a mere drop in the ocean to what Hogan knew he could make by carefully manipulating the difference in the price of gold to that of paper money. He had a twelve-month contract and knew that this would make him the richest man in Cooperville. Perhaps even the state.

The Mason silver mine paid him in gold and Hogan would pay their miners in paper. Totally legal. Unquestionably profitable.

The banker knew that he had to make another half-dozen stacks of paper money before his job was done.

It might take him all night but he did not care. Like an ancient moneylender Hogan kept on counting out the weathered paper greenbacks and ensuring the arithmetic matched the payroll figures. Each miner would get exactly what the book said they were owed.

They would not have a clue that they had actually been robbed.

Barton Hogan closed the safe door and locked it with a satisfied chuckle. The golden fortune in coins was now secure as far as he was concerned.

Or it might have been if it had not been for the five horsemen who had just entered the outskirts of Cooperville close by the livery stables at the other end of town.

Hogan did not have the slightest inkling that soon he too would know what it felt like to be robbed.

★   ★   ★

The deafening thunderclaps muffled the sound of the five horsemen as they

85

neared the tall building. Torrential rain swept over it as Grimes and his four followers dismounted and led their bedraggled horses out of the downpour into the livery. They paused as they studied the burly blacksmith seated close to one of the stalls, puffing on his pipe.

'Looks kinda big, don't he, boys,' Swift observed as he shook the rain from his soaked Stetson. He rested a thumb across his holstered .45.

'Nobody is big when a bullet hits their hearts, Stogey,' Grimes whispered knowingly. 'They die just as easy as normal-sized folks.'

'You want me to stable them nags for ya, gents?' Slim asked as he eased his bulk off the small stool and moved towards them past the tall-shouldered palomino, which was still standing tethered to the oak upright in the middle of the livery.

None of the five outlaws spoke.

They just watched as the huge blacksmith ambled towards them. The brawny figure seemed to have no interest in the men who had appeared out of the storm. He just looked at their soaked horses.

'I can bed and feed them for a dollar apiece,' Slim said, sucking the last of the smoke out of the tiny corn-cob bowl. Grimes moved away from the horses and watched as the big man turned to study him cautiously. 'You got any spare horse flesh for sale, big man?'

'Nope,' Slim answered. Suddenly he noticed the wooden peg as it emerged from Grimes's right pants leg. 'All these horses belong to folks in town. Ain't got no saddle horses.'

'But we want to buy five extra horses,' Grimes insisted.

'Sorry.' The blacksmith had his back to the others and continued to watch the outlaw leader as he hobbled to where the palomino stallion was standing.

'I'll have this 'un,' Grimes said in a low, cold tone. 'You can find us four others.'

Slim bit his lip. 'Are ya a bit deaf? I just told ya that none of these horses are for sale, mister.'

Grimes paused and looked at the huge man who was moving towards him. 'Then we'll just take them.'

The statement stunned the blacksmith.

'What?' Slim gasped.

Suddenly Cole moved forward and smashed the grip of one of his guns across the back of the blacksmith's head. Slim buckled and teetered around until he was facing his attacker. Then he staggered and raised his large hands. He reached out to grab hold of the ruthless outlaw's throat when Grimes hit him again with his own gun.

Blood sparkled as it flowed from the deep gashes in the back of the blacksmith's head. The hardened outlaws watched as the big man toppled like a felled tree. Slim crashed to the floor at their feet.

'Saddle five of these horses, Stogey,' Grimes ordered. 'You help him, Winston.'

The outlaw leader clung to the sides

of their bedraggled mounts for support as he made his way to the open doors. His cruel eyes stared out into the now raging storm. 'Make sure ya saddle that palomino. I'm having that 'un for myself.'

Grimes glanced at Brown as he carefully slid his hefty saddlebags off the back of his horse. He then turned to Cole and snapped his fingers.

'Help Dynamite carry them explosives, Laredo.' Grimes gave a smile. 'We got us a bank to gut and fillet.'

8

Swift and Parsons had hogtied the unconscious Slim and tethered him with a cutting rope to the tall oak upright in the centre of the livery stable. The two outlaws then went about saddling five extra horses as Grimes had ordered before he, Brown and Cole headed out into the driving rain to their inviting destination. Swift studied the powerful palomino and the Mexican saddle at its feet with envious eyes.

'This sure is one hell of a fancy rig,' he observed. Somehow he managed to lift the hefty saddle and throw it over the blanket on the stallion's back.

'And Peg Leg wants it all for himself, Stogey,' Parsons reminded him as he led another sturdy horse from its stall.

'Who in tarnation would own a critter as fine as this in these parts, Winston?' Swift asked. He drew the cinch straps under the horse's belly and secured them. 'Looks like the kinda horse a king or the like would ride.'

The youthful Parsons nodded in agreement. 'Yep. Reckon the dude that owns that horse is probably some sort of Mex royalty. Ya know the type?'

'Sure enough.' Swift sniffed. 'Bet he's as fancy as this here saddle. Bet he wears perfume and a powdered wig.'

Both men laughed.

Lightning forked down on all sides of Cooperville and momentarily lit up the entire town as the lethal rods of death sought and found their targets. Two exploding trees sent smouldering debris up into the relentless downpour of rain. The scent of burning defied the driving rain and wafted over the nervous settlement.

Some distance away in the unlit alleyways which ran behind every building on Main Street three figures moved ever closer to their goal. No storm, however devilish, could sway them from achieving what they had ridden fifty miles to do.

Few men with two legs could have moved as quickly through the deepening mud as Grimes did on his one. He was an expert with his crutch and used it to propel himself across the uneven ground at a pace neither Boston Brown or Laredo Cole could equal. The burly, thickset outlaw ignored the driving rain and worsening weather and moved quickly down the dark alleys behind the main thoroughfare.

Grimes had only one thought burning into his mind, and that was to get his hands on the veritable treasure which, his spies had informed him, had been delivered to Barton Hogan's bank only days earlier.

The rear of the bank had never had its integrity questioned in all the days since it had first been erected. Wooden walls set atop red-brick foundations might have been adequate for most buildings, but not those that needed to be secure.

The security of the rear door that led into the foyer of the bank at the side of

Hogan's private office was also questionable. It had never been tested in the twenty or so years since the door had first been hung on its frame. The rusted hinges and rotting panels should have been replaced at least a decade earlier, but Hogan was a man who liked to take other folks money and never spend his own.

The bedraggled Grimes stopped in the dismal alley and studied the rear door carefully. Even the darkness could not hide anything from eyes which were well used to peering into shadows. Cole reached him first with the saddle-bags of explosives and set them down beside the one-legged outlaw. It was a few moments before Brown caught up and rested a hand on the flaking panelled wall next to the door.

A flickering flash of light from helpful lightning illuminated the waterlogged alley just long enough for the three men to see what had to be done.

With his crutch still under his right armpit Grimes balanced and then pulled out a knife from his belt. He pushed the tip of its blade into the soft wood next to the hinges and began to loosen the screws away from the wall. It took barely two minutes for both hinges to come away from their wooden surround. The rusted screws fell silently into the mud at his feet.

'Laredo.' Grimes beckoned to his most deadly gunhand.

Cole knew what Grimes wanted. He gripped both sides of the door carefully and pulled it away from the frame.

Grimes watched as Cole turned, then placed the door against the alley fence behind them. The three outlaws entered the dark interior of the bank in single file.

They had gone barely two yards when Grimes raised his free hand and pointed to the office door to their right. The light of a lamp was showing beneath it. The outlaw gestured to both his men.

Cole drew one of his guns whilst Brown hung on to his hefty bag of dynamite sticks and fuses.

Grimes moved closer to the door and silently placed a hand on the brass doorknob. He looked at Cole, who hovered eagerly beside him.

The one-legged man pressed his ear next to the door and listened. He could hear the satisfied mutterings of the bank owner inside the office. Grimes turned the knob. Another deafening thunderclap exploded in the heavens above Cooperville. Every building in town shook.

The outlaw leader took full advantage. As the earth beneath their feet reverberated Grimes pushed the door open and gestured for Cole to run into the office with his gun held high.

Grimes and Brown followed the gunslinger.

A startled Barton Hogan looked up from the piles of cash in front of him and went to open a desk drawer next to his right thigh, but the outlaw had covered the distance from the office door to him far faster than Hogan had imagined possible.

Seeing the gun catching the lamp-light as it lay in the drawer, Cole lashed out and hit the banker across the face with the barrel of his own gun. Blood splattered across the room from Hogan's temple. He spun on his chair, then toppled to the boarded floor.

'Gotta be a hell of a lot faster than that, old man,' a satisfied Cole snarled down at the unconscious banker. He then looked at the table covered with carefully stacked piles of greenbacks and drooled. 'Holy cow. Is this what we come to steal, Peg Leg? There gotta be thousands of bucks here, all neatly stacked and waiting for us.'

'That ain't the fortune, Laredo.' Grimes hobbled to the tall safe and tried its door. It was locked up tight. 'The fortune is in here.'

Cole looked confused and pointed at the paper bills. 'But there must be ten thousand bucks here. What kinda fortune is in the safe?'

'Gold coin, boy,' Grimes snarled. He

stared down at the unconscious banker as blood flowed freely from his gashed head wound. 'Fresh-minted golden eagles. More than ya ever dreamed of seeing in one place, and they're locked up in the safe.'

'I'll find the key.' Cole was about to kneel down beside Hogan when Grimes grabbed his sleeve.

'Ain't no key will open that safe.'

Brown was studying the safe. 'Peg Leg is right. This safe's got a three-number tumbler. We have to have the combination to release its tumblers.'

'Damn it all, Laredo,' Grimes snorted angrily. 'Ya knocked out the only one of us that knows the combination of this damn thing.'

Cole shook his head. 'He ain't dead, Peg Leg. We could wake him up and make him tell us the numbers.'

Grimes stared at the safe and then at the two empty strongboxes on the floor. 'There ain't time. We gotta get out of this town long before sunup. We have to put a lot of ground between us and the posse. Our horses ain't gonna be travelling too fast with all that gold on their backs.'

Brown set his bags down and ran his hands over the steel door of the safe as though he were inspecting a desirable female. 'A Marsden 108. Made in New York. They don't make them no more. Lucky for us this is only a three-number tumbler and not the newer four and five versions.'

'What?' Cole gasped. 'What lingo is that ya spitting out there, Dynamite?'

Grimes rubbed his jaw and looked hard at Brown. 'Can ya open it, Dynamite?'

Brown gave a slow nod. 'Yeah but I'll have to blow the lock and that'll be mighty noisy.'

'Do it,' Grimes told Brown.

'Will we have time to fill them boxes before the town come swarming over us?' Cole asked Grimes anxiously. 'Even the smallest of explosions will be deafening, Peg Leg.'

Grimes grinned and pointed a finger

directly upward as yet again the heavens erupted in deafening fury. 'Not if we time it to match a thunderclap, Laredo. Folks will just think it's another blast of thunder.'

'Why don't we just take all the paper money?' Laredo Cole queried.

'You can fill ya pockets up with as much paper money as ya likes, boy,' Grimes told him. 'I'm still hankering to get me that gold coin.'

Brown knelt down and removed a long coiled fuse from his bags, together with a stick of dynamite. Both Cole and Grimes watched as Brown broke the stick of explosive in two and started to mould each piece in the palms of his hands. The pale outlaw looked up at Grimes.

'Ya sure ya want me to do this, Peg Leg?'

'Do it, Dynamite,' Grimes commanded. 'Do it good.'

9

A few seconds after a sheet of brilliant lightning had lit up the remote settlement the whole town shook as the loudest and most angered thunderclap vented its fury above Cooperville. Ancient gods were engaged in battle somewhere up in the dark sky and they would not cease their bitter conflict until someone or something below had also been destroyed.

The incessant rain continued driving down faster than the parched ground could absorb it. The streets were now awash in ankle-deep muddy water and troughs overflowed throughout the town. The tempest showed no sign of ceasing its bitter onslaught.

The smell of smoke filled the streets as burning trees dotted around the outskirts of the town were repeatedly hit by devilish bolts of unearthly indignation. The gods were once again showing their mortal underlings who was truly superior in the scheme of things.

Yet life carried on as normal for the hundreds of people who went about their nightly rituals regardless of what nature was inflicting upon them. Every one of the inhabitants of Cooperville realized that if your number was up there was little you could do about it. So the whiskey kept flowing and the tobacco smoke grew thicker.

With the body of Dan McGraw slung over one broad shoulder the sheriff was panting like an ancient hound dog by the time he had crossed the muddy street and reached the funeral parlour, which was set directly opposite the impressive bank. Welch kicked at the black-painted doors until the lamps inside broke into bright illumination around the door blinds.

The man who opened the door looked little better than his customers, with a pale complexion which seemed starved of life. Most men in Cooperville had a tan that matched their saddle leather, but not undertaker Wallace Culpepper.

Culpepper looked strange enough when dressed in his best funeral attire, but standing in his nightgown he appeared as though he had just paused haunting to answer the door.

'What you got there, Sheriff?' asked the frail-looking man as Welch pushed his way into the well-appointed front room of the funeral parlour.

'Where can I dump this bastard, Wally?' The sheriff spoke wheezily as sweat poured down from beneath his hatband. 'He's heavier than he looks. C'mon. Where can I dump this carcass?'

Culpepper closed the door and led the lawman to a long green-velvet drape. He opened the curtain and ushered the sheriff into the back room. This was where the gruesome business was done before bodies were nailed down into boxes.

'On the slab,' Culpepper said pointing at a marble block perched upon a solid wooden base. 'Put him down on there.'

There was a terrible stench in the back room of the funeral parlour which even the strongest of the undertaker's concoctions seemed unable to subdue.

'What's that smell, Wally?'

'Smell?' Culpepper seemed oblivious to it.

Welch eased the body off his shoulder on to the slab, then rested a hand upon the ice-cold surface. He was gasping for air as the thin man hovered over the body like a fly upon discovering a fresh dung pile.

'Ugly critter and no mistake,' the undertaker remarked. 'Where's his nose?'

'Well, I sure ain't got it.' The sheriff sighed and marched back out to where the fancy part of the premises was situated. Culpepper was on his tail.

'Business sure has bin good today, Jonas,' the undertaker said, rubbing his hands together.

The lawman paused by the door,

raised the blind and stared out into the driving rain which had hampered his journey across the muddy street. Then he glanced at the man shivering in his nightgown.

'Why don't ya light ya stove, Wally?'

Culpepper shook his head. 'No, no, no. That makes my guests ripen too quickly.'

'I guess it might at that. Send the bill to me, Wally.' Welch told him as he adjusted his gunbelt. 'Just don't make it too damn soon.'

'I surely will send you the bill.' The undertaker nodded as he opened the door. 'Coffins cost money. Can't be out of pocket in my business.'

'Reckon ya must be going to make a pretty penny when ya sell all them outlaws' guns and belts.' Welch stepped out into the fresh air and was thankful for the porch overhang. 'You must have made a tidy sum on all them outlaws I sent ya earlier.'

The thin man huffed, slammed the door shut behind the lawman and lowered the blind. The sheriff listened to bolts being slid into place behind the black door.

'Don't know why ya locking the door, Wally,' Welch shouted. 'Ain't as if anyone is gonna break in and steal anything.'

The lamplight was extinguished. The boardwalk fell into darkness as the sheriff turned to start his nightly rounds of the sprawling town. Then he paused as he caught a glimpse of a light glimmering around the blinds of the bank's front windows. Welch rubbed his chin.

'Barton must be working late,' he muttered to himself. Then he headed toward the nearest of the town's dozens of saloons.

Just as Welch was passing the double doors of the largest of Cooperville's many hotels he heard the clatter of boots above him on the veranda overhang. Fearing the worst the cautious sheriff drew his five-inch-barrelled Peacemaker and cocked its hammer in readiness for trouble. He was about to fire the weapon when the sound of large spurs mingling with the incessant pounding of the rain made him realize that it was the bounty hunter. Welch kept the gun trained on the sound as the familiar long legs came swinging over the lip of the porch.

Iron Eyes hung for a few seconds, then dropped down to the ground. He stood ankle-deep in mud as the lawman holstered his weapon.

'Ya almost give me heart failure, boy,' Welch said with a snort.

The bedraggled figure stepped up on to the boardwalk and ran his bony fingers through his wet hair. He briefly glanced up to the window from which he had just descended.

'That gal is loco, Sheriff,' Iron Eyes growled.

'She get frisky again?'

Iron Eyes nodded. 'She sure makes a man feared of getting himself some shut-eye and no mistake.'

'Was she putting her hands in ya

pockets again?' the sheriff asked as he began to walk with the strange figure at his side.

'Worse.' Iron Eyes swallowed hard.

'Ya want a drink, boy?' Sheriff Welch paused outside a saloon with the name of Broken Bottle painted on the wall next to its swing doors. The noise from inside the drinking hole seemed to calm the thin bounty hunter. 'Ya looks like a man that could sure use a few shots of whiskey.'

'I need me a whole bottle, old-timer.' Iron Eyes pushed the swing doors apart and led the lawman into the busy saloon. 'C'mon. I'm buying.'

The two men left sodden tracks in the sawdust as they made their way towards the bar counter made up of two large barrels topped by three-inch-thick pine boards.

The familiar sound of gasping disbelief filled both men's ears before they had even reached the crude bar counter.

A bartender of even greater girth

than the sheriff moved towards them and placed his hands on the counter.

'Whiskey?'

'Yep.' Iron Eyes nodded. 'Two bottles.'

'Two bottles?' Welch looked up at the mutilated face which showed no emotion as it stared around the room.

'Don't fret none, Sheriff. I'm paying.' Iron Eyes aimed a finger at the best-looking bottles behind the bartender and tossed a few silver dollars at the man. 'That cover it?'

'Yep.'

Iron Eyes grabbed both bottles. 'C'mon, Sheriff. I'm too damn tuckered to stand.'

The sheriff trailed the exhausted bounty hunter through the crowd until they found a dark corner of the Broken Bottle beneath a staircase that led to where the soiled doves earned their money. Iron Eyes sat down facing the room and placed the bottles before them on a card table. Welch sat next to Iron Eyes, grabbed one of the bottles and pulled its cork. Hidden by the shadows Iron Eyes remained bolt upright, watching all those who had been watching him.

'Ya seem awful interested in these critters,' Welch said after taking a low slow swig.

'Just checking out their faces,' Iron Eyes whispered. 'I sure don't want to have another damn outlaw trying his luck. I'm too damn tuckered.'

'Ain't ya gonna open your bottle, boy?'

'When I'm good and ready, old-timer,' the bounty hunter replied. He adjusted both his Navy Colts so that their grips were jutting out away from his belt. 'When I'm sure no one has a hankering to kill me I'll take me a drink.'

'Relax,' the sheriff said with a sigh.

'Folks in my profession tend to die awful fast when they relax, old-timer.' Iron Eyes dragged the bottle off the table and plucked the cork from its neck with his teeth. He spat the cork across the saloon and raised the bottle neck to his scarred lips.

'That little gal has got ya spooked,

boy,' the sheriff remarked with an amused smile. 'Most men would have had their way with anything as young and tender as her. How old is she, exactly?'

'Damned if I know,' Iron Eyes drawled. 'Hell, I don't rightly know how old I am.'

The whiskey burned a welcome path down the throat of the bounty hunter. He let out a long breath, then placed the bottle back on the table.

'She sure has made it damn hard for me to get any shut-eye.'

The lawman leaned closer to his companion. 'Where do ya intend sleeping tonight if ya don't go back to the hotel?'

'In one of ya cells, or maybe even here,' Iron Eyes replied in a low dry tone. 'I can hardly keep awake as it is.'

The more whiskey the sheriff poured down his neck the more he started to notice the bar girls who were roaming around the saloon's menfolk in search of their next willing customer. Most of the females who had witnessed Iron Eyes enter the Broken Bottle seemed too afraid of the hideous stranger to venture anywhere near the table beneath the stairs.

Then, just as Welch heard footsteps descending the stairs above their heads, he also heard the soft snoring sound coming from Iron Eyes. The lawman turned his head and saw something that surprised him. The bounty hunter was fast asleep, but his eyes remained wide open behind the limp hair which hung before his mutilated features. Welch was about to awaken the deadly hunter when he heard his name being spoken.

'Well if it ain't Jonas.'

Welch glanced up and saw one of the saloon's favourite and better looking whores staring down at them. It had been her footsteps he had heard coming down from another ten minutes hard labour.

'Polly.' The sheriff touched the brim of his hat.

'Jonas, baby.' Pecos Polly purred as she stood just beyond the edge of the card table. 'It sure is a long time since I seen you in here. Ya got the itch, big boy? Remember how I made that itch feel so good?'

'I sure do, Polly.' Welch gulped.

She snatched the bottle from his hands and took herself a few big gulps of the fiery liquor. 'Damn! That sure is mighty fine rye.'

'My pal bought it.' Welch gestured to the sleeping bounty hunter who appeared to be looking directly at her. The shadows hid most of his face but not the eyes. Polly could see them quite clearly apparently returning her gaze.

Never one to run the risk of losing a potential customer to her fellow bar girls, Polly placed the bottle down, bent over and took hold of the hem of her heavily petticoat-layered dress. She hoisted it up under her chin to reveal her naked form and wiggled her assets.

'Like what ya see, stranger?' she vainly asked.

Sheriff Welch drooled at the sight of her bare flesh. Flesh he had tasted many times. 'I see ya still ain't got around to buying no underpants, Polly gal.'

She laughed and kept on shaking her dress like a matador trying to tempt a bull to charge. 'C'mon, stranger. Take a good look at Pecos Polly. Ya can have an even closer look if ya got the price. What ya say? Ya wanna take Polly upstairs?'

Her untrimmed femininity at the top of her still fine legs moved as Polly gyrated her supple hips expertly just above the top of the table beyond its green baize. Welch leaned closer and sighed heavily.

'What ya say, stranger?' Polly raised her voice and then glanced at the sheriff. 'He ain't dead is he, Jonas?'

'Iron Eyes.' Welch nudged the arm of the slumbering bounty hunter and noticed that the sound of snoring stopped as quickly as it had started. 'Look.'

The yawning bounty hunter inhaled deeply, then blinked hard as his tired eyes tried to focus. He caught sight of the bar girl's attributes moving less than three feet from where he was seated. He jolted backwards either in shock or surprise before jumping to his feet.

Faster than either the lawman or Pecos Polly could even blink the drowsy Iron Eyes's right hand went for the grip of one of his guns. He drew and cocked the Navy Colt in one fluid action and aimed its lethal barrel straight across the table.

'No, Iron Eyes. Don't shoot,' Welch yelled out, forcing the gun barrel down just as its trigger was squeezed by the bony finger. Tufts of green baize and splinters erupted as the bullet went through the table and into the floor.

'What ya doing?' Welch yelled out.

Pecos Polly screamed, dropped her petticoats and ran for her life into the crowd.

The sound of his gun firing woke Iron Eyes. He turned and looked at the sheriff who was still holding on to the barrel of the Navy Colt.

'Why'd ya stop me?' Iron Eyes asked.

'I had to, boy.'

'Didn't ya see it?' The weary bounty hunter yawned.

The sheriff released his grip. 'See what?'

'There was a rat on the table, Sheriff.' Iron Eyes sighed heavily and pointed. 'A stinking rat right there.'

The sheriff raised his eyebrows. 'It weren't no rat, boy.'

Iron Eyes grabbed his bottle, swilled another mouthful of whiskey around his tongue and teeth, then swallowed. He leaned forward and rested a hand on the table top.

'If it weren't a rat then what in tarnation was it?'

'It don't matter none.' Welch shook his head.

'And why'd that bar gal scream out like that?' Iron Eyes yawned again. 'Maybe she saw that rat as well.'

'That must be it, boy. That and ya scaring the life out of her by firing this hogleg.' Welch picked up his own bottle from the green baize. He took a swig and stood up. 'C'mon. Reckon we ought to go to my office and let ya finish ya sleep in one of my cells.'

'Sounds OK.' Dog-tired, Iron Eyes allowed the older man to guide him across the saloon. They headed towards the swing doors and the street. 'Ya know something that troubles me?'

'What?'

'How come Squirrel Sally is so interested in me?' Iron Eyes dropped his bottle into his trail-coat pocket and leaned down. 'I sure ain't the prettiest critter around. It don't make no sense.'

'Maybe Squirrel has real poor eyesight,' Welch suggested.

Iron Eyes nodded. 'That might be it, but she sure can shoot damn well for someone with bad eyes.'

'Some folks are just plumb lucky when it comes to shooting at other critters, boy.' Welch led the tired bounty hunter out into the street. 'On the other hand maybe she just likes ugly men.'

Iron Eyes gave out a short brief laugh.

'Damn it all. I finally found an honest lawman.'

Sheriff Welch moved to the edge of the boardwalk and held out a hand. 'At least it's stopped raining.'

'The storm ain't quit, though.'

'Old Barton must be still counting his money over yonder, boy,' Welch noted. He pointed at the light escaping from around the bank's window blinds.

'Counting my reward money,' Iron Eyes corrected.

The sky rumbled noisily once again. It sounded like a hundred Apache war drums being pounded at exactly the same time. The two men stepped down into the wet street and started to try and navigate across its width.

With boots being sucked into the muddy water they made slow progress. They had barely reached the middle of the wide street when another roaring noise erupted.

They paused and looked up.

But this deafening explosion was not coming from above. It was the sound of dynamite blasting open a large safe directly opposite them.

Suddenly the windows of the bank shattered into a million fragments as they were blown out. Even the frames of the windows were propelled out into the dark street. Amid the smoke and debris deadly glass shards flew out like crystal daggers from the bank.

It was as though they had been charged by a rampaging bull. Everything that had been blown out of the bank seemed to hit them full on. Smouldering wooden splinters and particles of glass hidden by choking smoke hit them hard. The brutal force of the powerful explosion knocked both startled men off their feet and flung them backwards.

Two plumes of muddy water rose into the air around the pair of battered men.

Squirrel Sally raced out on to the veranda of the hotel with her trusty Winchester in her small hands and gasped in amazement at the sight below her. Billowing smoke had filled the street from the guts of the shattered bank opposite. She stared down in horror at the sight of the two men stretched out in the mud and water. Even the street lanterns could not hide the blood from her knowing eyes. Then another equally astonishing sight caught her attention. At first it appeared as though a million fireflies were filling the street with their bright dancing lights but these were not fireflies, she told herself. This was money. Burning paper money. The air was filled with it. It was raining paper money and each banknote was alight from the blast which had destroyed the front of the bank and spewed the stacked piles of greenbacks out into the night air.

There were other things scattered all across the waterlogged street and she stared down at them before focusing on the familiar figure of the stunned bounty hunter lying next to the sheriff.

'Iron Eyes,' she shrieked out loudly. 'No.'

Neither the bounty hunter nor the lawman answered her desperate call. Neither of them moved as the water began to drag them down beneath its muddy surface.

Squirrel Sally clambered over the rail and then leapt.

10

She was like a mountain cat: fast and silent as she hit the soft muddy ground with her Winchester clutched in her small hands. Yet Squirrel Sally Cooke wanted to scream even louder than she had done a few heartbeats earlier. The sight of the long-legged bounty hunter spilling blood from a thousand wounds made her remember discovering her dead family only a very few days before. Iron Eyes had become her entire world. If she had now lost him as well she dreaded what remained of her existence. He did not know it, but he had become her only reason to live.

Leaving her rifle on the boardwalk propped up against a wooden upright Squirrel Sally waded out in her bare feet through the ice-cold water and mud to the pair of silent figures who were sinking fast.

'Iron Eyes,' she frantically blazed into

his ear. There was no response. 'Ya better not be dead, ya stupid bastard. I'll kill ya if ya are.'

Squirrel looked at the sheriff. He was grunting each time his head sank beneath the surface of the flooded street. 'Wake up, Sheriff. Wake up, ya fat old man.'

Like the bounty hunter beside him Jonas Welch seemed totally unable to do anything except drown.

'Reckon I'd better get ya both on to them boards yonder.' She grabbed the collar of the sheriff and gripped the mane of long black hair floating above Iron Eyes's submerged head. The tiny female wrapped the hair around her wrist and hauled both men's heads out of their watery graves. Using the water to float her burdens Squirrel dragged them across the surface of the knee-deep water. The mud sucked at her tiny feet but she was determined to achieve her goal. Squirrel did not stop until she had reached the steps leading up to the boardwalk.

A crowd of men had gathered to

watch the spectacle.

None ventured down from the board-walk to assist the struggling female, however.

Mustering every ounce of her strength Squirrel Sally heaved the hefty lawman up and rested his bulk against the steps. Sheriff Welch was riddled with countless shards of glass and wood and bleeding like a stuck pig from nearly every wound. She patted his head as he lay coughing and then turned to the bounty hunter. Iron Eyes seemed to be lifeless but she had seen him that way before.

She took hold of his mane of black hair and pulled his thin body up until it rested next to the lawman. Unlike Welch the bounty hunter was entirely motionless. A large dagger-shaped piece of glass was stuck in his thin shoulder. Blood squirted from around the injury. Without even thinking Squirrel pulled the glass out of his flesh, tossed it aside, then pressed her small hand on to the wound. Blood trickled from the gaps in her fingers.

Both men had been pierced with count-less bits of debris. They looked like porcupines. Frantically the young female began to pull the brutal fragments of wood and glass from Iron Eyes's body.

Her gaze burned up at the onlookers. 'Somebody better go bring a doctor here damn fast or I'll kill ya all.'

Blood ran freely from both men's wounds as one of the watchers turned and seemed to be obeying her angry order.

Then a well-attired man moved away from the crowd and leaned over the kneeling Squirrel Sally. He rested a hand on her slender shoulder.

'Leave him be, boy. Ya wasting ya time,' the man said. 'He's dead.'

A fire was suddenly ignited in her belly. Like a rabid hound Squirrel got to her feet and glared at the man with blazing eyes. With bloody hands she snatched her Winchester from where it rested and mounted the last few steps. With the barrel of the rifle aimed at his groin the man backed away until he was standing in front of what remained of one of the hotel's windows.

'What ya say, dude?' Squirrel snarled, poking the rifle into his manhood.

'I said for you to leave him be, boy.' The man made the mistake of repeating himself. 'He's obviously dead.'

'One, I ain't no boy. Two, I'm a gal.' Squirrel swung her hips and kicked the man viciously between the legs with every scrap of her strength. He buckled, as all men tend to do when feet find their weakness. As his head came down she kneed him powerfully in his jaw. The sound of teeth cracking filled the air. She then brought the rifle stock up. He was knocked off his feet and flew backwards. She watched the well-dressed man as he went flying through the shattered window. An open-mouthed hotel clerk twitched as the man landed at his feet.

Squirrel Sally raised a finger and pointed it at the dazed man. 'Three, Iron Eyes ain't dead. He always looks like that.'

Welch spluttered and then coughed.

'What happened?'

A snarling Squirrel looked at the stunned audience which had just witnessed her losing her temper. 'Get a damn doctor or I'll blow all ya worthless heads clean off. Savvy?'

At least half of the onlookers did exactly as she had ordered and ran to find the town's only doctor.

Squirrel stared down at the still motionless Iron Eyes. Her heart was racing as the dude's words ran through her mind. She crouched and placed her hand back on the most serious of the bleeding wounds.

'Ya better not be dead, ya bastard,' she growled.

'What happened, Squirrel gal?' the sheriff asked as he managed to sit upright.

'That building yonder blew up,' she answered.

'The bank?' Welch coughed again, and then started to pull glass from his chest and legs.

Squirrel knelt and kept staring at the

lifeless form of the bounty hunter. Then she cast her eyes upon the lawman. 'He ain't dead, is he, Sheriff?'

Welch could hear the concern in her trembling voice as he edged closer to Iron Eyes. He swallowed hard as he saw all the blood which was running from a multitude of wounds. He hesitated and gulped.

'Is he or ain't he?' Squirrel growled.

'I don't know, gal,' Welch admitted. 'I ain't no sawbones but I sure need me one.'

A troubled Squirrel breathed hard. She narrowed her eyes.

'Who done this?'

Still dazed, Welch blinked hard and felt the small cuts which covered his face. 'I ain't sure, gal. Someone must have bin robbing the bank, I guess.'

'Reckon they used too much dynamite by the looks of it.'

'Looks that way,' the sheriff agreed.

Suddenly, without warning, Squirrel stood up and cranked the hand guard of her rifle, sending a spent casing flying over her shoulder. She growled. 'And them varmints killed my Iron Eyes.'

'W-what?' Welch looked at her. 'We don't know that for sure, gal.'

'That fancy dude was right, ya stupid fat old critter.' She sniffed. 'He's dead. Now I'm gonna have to go find and kill them bank robbers. Learn 'em a lesson they'll never forget.'

The sheriff tried to reach her with an outheld hand but failed. 'Easy, gal. Like ya said, Iron Eyes always looks like this. I reckon he's just bin knocked out.'

'Iron Eyes is dead,' Squirrel Sally said. Tears flowed down her cheeks. 'And I'm on my lonesome again. Somebody is gonna pay high for that. Mark my words, old man. They're gonna pay high.'

'Don't go jumping the gun, Squirrel gal.' Welch placed a hand on the bounty hunter's chest and desperately tried to feel a heartbeat. All he could feel was blood seeping from the countless cuts. 'Wait for the doc.'

Squirrel no longer heard anything. 'They must have hightailed it through the back lanes, Sheriff. Nobody come out the front way. They must have left their nags at the edge of town.'

'So what?' Welch coughed. 'This ain't nothing for you to fret about. This is my business.'

She still did not hear him. 'They gotta be headed for their horses. Where would a gang of bank robbers leave their nags in a storm?'

'The livery,' Welch heard himself answer.

'Damn right.' Squirrel Sally nodded and glanced up and down the long street. 'I need me a horse.'

A couple of curious cowboys were riding along the street, drawn by the sound of the massive explosion. As one of the riders passed the hotel Squirrel jumped on to the rim of the water trough, then leapt on to the long hitching rail and threw herself at the horseman. The cowboy was hit by her leading foot and went tumbling off his

129

saddle just as the small female replaced him on the high-shouldered pinto. Even though her feet did not reach the stirrups it did not hamper her. Squirrel pulled the reins up to her chin and kicked back with her feet.

'I'm going to the livery,' she announced as the horse responded to its new mistress.

The sheriff had no time to say a word. The horse and rider started down towards the distant livery. Only the soft mud of the street slowed its progress.

Suddenly Iron Eyes groaned and then sat uptight. He rubbed his bleeding face and stared at the small female on the tall pinto. Then he glanced at the lawman. 'What's Squirrel doing?'

The man with the star pinned to his vest gasped. 'Damn it all. Ya ain't dead.'

'I know that, ya old fool.' Iron Eyes slapped the sheriff across the face. 'Answer me. Where's Squirrel going?'

'She's gone to tackle them bank robbers,' Welch replied. 'She figures they must be heading for the livery.'

'She's right.' The bounty hunter

stood and beckoned to the other cowboy who steered his gelding close to the hotel steps.

The cowboy rested an elbow on the horn of his saddle, leaned over the neck of his mount and stared down at the thin figure covered from head to toe in gore. 'What ya want, handsome?'

Never taking his ice-cold eyes off the pinto as it travelled down the street, Iron Eyes grabbed the cowboy's bandanna and jerked it hard. The cowboy went over the shoulder of the bounty hunter and landed in the trough.

Sheriff Welch watched Iron Eyes swing up on to the saddle and then drive his huge spurs mercilessly into the flesh of the horse. It reared up, then galloped after the pinto.

'Did they just steal our horses, Sheriff?' one of the cowboys asked the lawman.

'Damned if I know, son.'

11

The brawny blacksmith blinked and opened his eyes. His skull felt as though it had been crushed by the merciless blows of his attackers. Slim lay on his side and began to move. Only then did he realize that his feet and arms were tethered. Ignoring the pain which filled his throbbing head the large man tilted his head and stared at the two men who were bathed in the glowing red light of the forge. Slim gritted his teeth and tried to flex his mighty arms in an attempt to break his bonds.

Oblivious to the fact that the blacksmith had awoken from his enforced slumber, outlaws Stogey Swift and Winston Parsons led the last of the ten horses out of the livery and tied their reins to the long whitewashed corral poles next to the building. Each horse was saddled and ready. Like everyone else in Cooperville, the pair of outlaws had felt the ground shake beneath their boots when the unexpectedly violent explosion had rocked the town to its shallow foundations.

Both men knew something had not gone to plan, but they had continued doing what Grimes had ordered them to do.

A sudden lightning flash in the sky above the two outlaws highlighted the cloud of black smoke which had erupted from the bank when the dynamite had exploded. Now that the storm was abating it hung over Cooperville like a disgruntled genie after escaping from a magic lamp.

Both outlaws knew that they would soon discover what had happened or what was about to happen. Soon they would have the answers to all the questions their anxious minds were posing.

Swift patted the magnificent palomino stallion, then ran with Parsons back into the stable.

They knew that instead of greeting their three comrades returning with their loot, they might be faced with a crowd of hostile guns. Guns which would unleash the fury that only the righteous have in abundance. For all they knew all the able-bodied gun-toting men in town might soon be converging on them.

'I sure don't like this, Stogey.' Parsons drew one of his Colts and knelt next to the bewhiskered Swift, who was cradling a rifle in his hands. They were staring through the gap between one of the high stable doors and its weathered frame.

'That sure was one hell of a big bang,' Swift said as sweat trailed down his face. 'I reckon something went wrong.'

Parsons swallowed hard. 'Yeah. Boston must have used too much dynamite and not enough fuse.'

Set on a slightly higher elevation than the rest of the town the high-walled livery was shrouded in the blackest of shadows and offered them unchallenged views of anyone approaching.

With their rifles cocked and ready Swift and Parsons waited.

Then the sound of horses snorting as they made their way through the muddy streets filled both outlaws' ears.

'Hear that, Stogey?' Parsons asked, screwing up his eyes and peering out from the livery.

'Yep. I hear it.'

'Riders.'

'Sure enough. Now cock that hogleg, boy,' Swift advised his young companion as he poked the barrel of his rifle out into the night air. 'Somebody is coming and it ain't none of our boys.'

Three-quarters of the way along the main street Iron Eyes mercilessly whipped the shoulders of the gelding as the straining animal tried to outrun the pain being inflicted upon it by the desperate bounty hunter. The brutal spurs continued to thrust their sharp points into the horse's flesh until Iron Eyes drew level with the pinto.

Lightning flashed high above the town as Squirrel Sally saw the unholy face of the man who, only moments earlier, she had thought was dead.

At the corner of a side street and the livery stable she drew rein. The bounty hunter hauled the mane of his mount back and leapt from the saddle. He landed just ahead of both snorting horses. He raised his hands and stopped the pinto from advancing another stride.

'Hold on there, little 'un,' the gaunt figure called up to the stunned female.

Squirrel steadied the pinto and stared in disbelief at the bounty hunter as his bony hands pulled both his Navy Colts from his belt and pulled back on their hammers.

She jumped from the saddle and ran to his side.

'I thought ya was a goner,' she blurted out.

Iron Eyes did not reply. He gathered the reins of both horses, led them in between two buildings and secured their leathers to a porch upright.

'How come ya ain't dead?' Sally shouted at the man who was still bleeding from the countless cuts on his body.

He paused and glanced down at her.

'I am Iron Eyes. I take a whole lotta killing, gal.'

Before she could respond the bounty hunter pushed her aside, edged to the corner of the side street and looked up at the outline of the livery. Standing slightly higher than the rest of Cooperville the building loomed like a watchful monster. The sky rumbled as Iron Eyes studied the livery with knowing eyes.

'Why'd ya stop here?' Squirrel asked.

'Coz I ain't hankering to get shot,' Iron Eyes replied. He continued to look hard at the livery cloaked in black shadow. 'That's why.'

She rested the stock of her Winchester on her hip and tried to see whatever it was that his keen eyesight had already noticed.

'What ya looking at, Iron Eyes?' She had to ask at last.

'Can't ya see them?'

'See what?'

Slowly Iron Eyes raised one of his guns and pointed just beyond the wide-open doors of the building. Squirrel Sally edged a couple of steps closer before he dragged her back.

'Horses,' the bounty hunter snarled. 'A whole heap of the critters by that corral fence. And that ain't all.'

Then the flicking of tails drew her youthful attention to the very place at which her companion was aiming one of his deadly guns.

'I see 'em.' She sighed. 'Six or seven of them.'

'Ten,' Iron Eyes corrected without moving a muscle. 'And one of them horses is my stallion. Them varmints are figuring on stealing my horse.'

Squirrel could hear the anger in his voice. 'I don't see me no bank robbers, though.'

'That's why I'm troubled, little 'un.'

'What ya mean?'

'I don't see any of them outlaws either, and there sure has to be a few of the critters around here someplace.'

Iron Eyes poked one of his guns back into his pants belt and then reached into his pocket. He plucked from it some of the broken glass of his whiskey bottle and discarded it. 'Damn. There was a good half-pint of rye left in that bottle.'

She watched him licking his fingers. 'They must still be in town or they'd have taken the horses. Right?' she offered.

'Yep.' His eyes darted to her and then returned to the livery.

'Why'd they want so many horses? Do ya figure there might be ten of them outlaw varmints?' She swallowed hard. 'Do ya?'

Iron Eyes did not answer her question. He nudged her elbow with his own, then silently made his way towards a large-trunked tree where the shadows were even denser. She tracked his every step.

The sky above them rumbled as the last remnants of the storm passed overhead. A few fleeting wisps of bright light flickered off in the distance, but both Iron Eyes and Squirrel Sally knew that the storm had not truly ended. Not the one which they felt still lay in wait somewhere near the livery.

Then they saw them. Three figures emerged from the alley directly across from the wide-open doors of the livery stable. At first the shadows almost hid them from sight but then Grimes, Cole and Brown came fully into view. The bounty hunter rose to his full height as he watched the men carrying hefty money-bags between them. He instinctively knew by the effort the men were displaying that the bags must be fully laden with gold.

The excited female raised her rifle to her shoulder.

Iron Eyes shook his head. 'No.'

'Why not? I could pick them off easy,' she said.

He leaned close. 'How'd we know they're the critters we're after, gal? They could be anyone.'

Squirrel Sally looked startled. 'I thought ya shot anyone ya damn well liked, Iron Eyes.'

A crooked smile appeared from behind the mask of blood which covered his face.

'I only kill vermin with bounty on their heads.'

Suddenly without warning two ear-splitting shots rang out from the gap in the tall livery doors. Then bullets cut into the tree beside them. Chunks of bark showered over both Iron Eyes and Sally. Then another volley of shots pealed out in quick succession. The two watchers threw themselves on to the ground and returned fire just as the three men vanished from sight behind the large stable doors.

'Now ya can kill as many of them as ya like, little 'un.' Iron Eyes snarled from the corner of his twisted mouth as he blasted bullets towards the telltale signs of gunsmoke.

Squirrel Sally pushed down the hand guard on her rifle and then spat to her side as she lay outstretched beside the bounty hunter. 'Great. Now that I can shoot 'em I can't see the bastards no more, ya dumb galoot.'

Bullet after bullet shot forth from the long seven-inch barrel of his Navy Colt but he heard no hint of any of the lethal projectiles finding their targets.

Choking gunsmoke lingered a few feet above the ground and made their targets even harder to see.

'They got us pinned down here,' Sally snarled as she fired her carbine three times in quick sequence.

'No, they ain't,' Iron Eyes contradicted her. Defiantly he scrambled back to his feet. 'We got them pinned down, gal. They're trapped inside that barn.'

'Where ya going?' she asked as she too managed to rise to her feet next to him.

'Just follow me,' Iron Eyes instructed.

The tiny female did as she was told and trailed the fast-moving bounty hunter as his long thin legs cut across the muddy ground towards a store with the word 'Printers' painted on its façade. Fiery lead blazed after them through the cold night air from the confines of the livery. The wall of the printer's office kicked out sawdust as most of the outlaws' bullets hit its corner. Iron Eyes and Squirrel Sally dropped down into the mud behind an overflowing trough. With rifle bullets still carving chunks of wood off the wall behind them, they reloaded.

'Wait for them to quit shooting before ya fire back,' Iron Eyes whispered in his low rasping voice. 'Wait for them to reload. Savvy?'

'Why the hell did we come over here, Iron Eyes?' Sally shouted as a half-dozen more bullets slugged into the trough, causing plumes of water to splash over the pair of them. 'Least we was dry over yonder.'

'We got us a damn better chance of picking the varmints off from here, gal,' he answered. He drew his second Colt from his belt and hauled back on its hammer. 'And this trough will stop their bullets from hitting us.'

More of the outlaws' shots hit the

trough. Water rose into the air and then came crashing over them again.

'We're gonna drown, though,' Sally snorted. She leaned around the trough, levelled her Winchester and fired. For the first time they heard the sound of a man yelping. 'Damn it all. I hit me one of them.'

'Lucky.' Iron Eyes rose, blasted half a dozen shots before dropping back down next to her.

'I hit one of them,' she repeated.

'So what? Ya shot me a week or so back.' The bounty hunter was looking up at the glass of the office window above them, trying to make sense of the reflection it displayed.

'What ya looking at?' she asked curiously.

'I'm trying to see where they are by the flashes of their guns, Squirrel,' Iron Eyes replied. He pointed at the window.

Then the window was hit by a salvo of at least a score of bullets. Glass shattered and fell over them.

She pushed her lips to his ear.

'Reckon they heard ya.'

The inside of the livery was filled with gunsmoke as Parsons grabbed hold of Swift's shoulder and shook him. The rifle fell from the older outlaw's lifeless hands.

'They got Stogey, Peg Leg,' Parsons blurted out in shock. 'Killed him good and dead.'

Grimes was forcing bullets into the magazine of his rifle as both Cole and Brown kept firing their weaponry at the trough. He gritted his teeth then exhaled loudly.

'Damn it all. He's the only one that knows the trail past Red Pepper.'

Parsons moved over to Grimes. 'Then how we gonna get home?'

'Reckon we ain't gonna get no place unless we stop them *hombres* from shooting at us, Winston boy,' Grimes growled. His keen mind raced as he tried to find an answer. He turned to Cole and tapped the barrel of his rifle against the deadly killer's shoulder. 'Are them bags of gold secured on the horses, Laredo?'

Cole gave a slow nod as he kept firing at the trough. 'Yep. I made sure that they're double hogtied, Peg Leg.'

'Good.' Grimes nodded. 'We don't want any of them bags we filled with coin falling off the backs of these nags.'

'But how we gonna get away from here?' Parsons asked. Speedily he pushed bullets into the smoking chambers of his guns. 'Ya already said them varmints got us trapped. If'n we turn our backs to mount our horses they'll fill us with lead.'

Grimes looked at the dejected Brown. His lips curled in anger. 'This is all Dynamite's damn fault.'

Brown glanced up at the brooding outlaw. 'OK. I used too much dynamite. That safe looked a whole lot tougher than it was.'

'Ya almost killed us,' Grimes snarled.

'And ya woke up the whole town,' Cole added.

'Them town folks would not have known we had blown their bank's safe if ya had done the job right.' Grimes spat. 'And we wouldn't be stuck in this dung heap trying to fight our way out of town.'

Brown got to his feet and rested his back against the wall beside the one-legged man. The red light from the forge lit up his face. It was the face of a dying man. 'I'm sorry. Ya right, this is all my fault, Peg Leg. I just ain't feeling right no more.'

There was no compassion in the stocky Grimes. He grabbed the shirt collar of the crestfallen Brown and pulled it close to his cruel face. 'Then listen up. It's up to you to figure a way of getting us out of here before more gun-happy critters come to join them two bastards yonder. Now think of something. If'n ya don't we'll all end up like Stogey. Rich dead 'uns.'

Parsons knelt next to Cole and began to fire across the wide muddy expanse to where Iron Eyes and his tiny attendant were still huddled behind the trough. But even as the gunfire grew more deafening inside the livery none of them noticed that the huge black-smith was no longer where they had left him. Inch by inch Slim had moved away from the oak upright towards the glowing forge where the burly man kept his tools. Tools with which he knew he could cut through his bonds and free himself.

Behind the trough, as more and more bullets pierced its weathered sides, Iron Eyes got on to his knees and gritted his teeth angrily. 'Damn it all. I'm wasting lead here. Ain't no profit in missing ya targets, ya know.'

'I hit one of them,' Sally said smugly. 'How come ya keep missing, ya galoot? Them eyes of yours playing up again?'

Iron Eyes glared at her through his limp strands of hair and then, to her surprise, smiled. 'Reckon ya as painful as a bullet in the rump, Squirrel.'

As the shooting paused for a few brief moments Iron Eyes and Squirrel jumped to their feet and opened up with guns and rifle. Red tapers of deadly lead spewed from their weapons' barrels and cut through the shadows towards the livery. But for some reason there was no response. The bank robbers appeared to have gone.

Somehow they had melted into the shadows.

'Where are they?' Squirrel wondered. 'Where in tarnation did they go, Iron Eyes?'

The bounty hunter pushed both his guns into his pants belt, grabbed hold of her soaked shirt and hauled her back down behind the cover of the trough.

'They're still in there someplace,' came the low, chilling reply. The thin man shook the spent brass casings from his hot guns and reloaded with bullets from his coat's deep pockets.

Squirrel Sally sat with the rifle across her lap and toyed with her ripped shirt. 'Look what ya done.'

'I stopped ya from getting ya head shot off, gal,' Iron Eyes mumbled. Then he looked at where she was pointing: at her exposed, mud-covered breasts. 'Oh.'

'No wonder I done shot ya,' Squirrel snorted. 'Ya just can't keep ya hands off my chest.'

Before Iron Eyes could say another word another barrage of hot lead came at them. Wood splinters and water flew up like crashing waves as the trough began to disintegrate under the incessant impacts.

'I told ya they weren't gone,' the bounty hunter said.

The deafening blasts echoed all about the area as the crouching pair waited for another lull in the bombardment to return fire.

'They sure are mighty mad, Iron Eyes.' Squirrel coughed as more and more water showered over them.

'I don't give a damn. All I wanna do is kill 'em all.' Iron Eyes looked to his side. He saw the gap beneath the building next to him and crawled through the mud until he was under the boardwalk outside the front of the printer's office. He could hear Squirrel cursing as she followed him. Then the barrel of her Winchester came up next to his head. He brushed it aside.

'Careful with that damn carbine,' he warned her, and looked out at the front of the livery. It was dark inside the big building. Only the familiar red glow from the forge shed any light inside it.

'Can ya see 'em?'

The bounty hunter did not answer her. Iron Eyes just waited for the next volley of shots to light up the darkness and tell him exactly where they were. Then his own silent question was answered. To his surprise none of the outlaws seemed to be inside the livery. They were close to the horses, where they had already tied the bags of golden coins to the saddle cantles.

'They're by the nags,' Iron Eyes said out of the corner of his mouth.

'Them yella bellies must be ready to hightail it.'

Suddenly Cole and Parsons started to unload bullets from between some of the horses. The shots skimmed across the top of the trough.

151

'They're right next to my horse,' Iron Eyes growled. 'Them stinking varmints are using my palomino as a damn shield.'

More of the outlaws' bullets hit the wall of the office.

'Why don't ya fire if ya can see 'em?' she nagged into his ear, then crawled over his legs and pushed the barrel of her rifle past his face. 'I'll shoot the critters.'

Sally squeezed her trigger and sent a shot into the group of tethered horses. One of the animals made a hideous sound, then crashed down on to the muddy ground. Iron Eyes grabbed the hot rifle barrel and looked at her.

'Ya young fool,' he scolded.

'What's wrong?'

Then the answer became obvious. Her shot had alerted the outlaws to the fact that their targets had moved position. Now both Cole and Parsons knew where to aim and fire their weaponry.

Before Iron Eyes had time to fire his guns again he saw the bank robbers turn their weapons on him. A blinding fusillade of bullets rained down on the pair as they desperately slid back through the mud to the relative safety of the trough.

Mud kicked up all over the thin man as he shielded Sally from the deadly lead.

'Why didn't ya shoot 'em?' she asked.

'They're by the horses, Squirrel.' Iron Eyes tried to explain as he plucked the spent shells from his guns and replaced them with fresh bullets.

She swung around, cranked her rifle and fired over the trough lip again.

Angrily Iron Eyes pulled her down again into the mud and water. 'Don't go shooting at them there, gal. My horse is over there.'

She looked at him with mud dripping off her face and chest.

'So?'

He pushed his bleeding face close to hers and raised both his scarred eyebrows. 'I likes that horse. Savvy?'

'Do ya like that horse as much as ya

likes me, Iron Eyes?' She purred like a kitten and then provocatively rubbed the mud off her pert breasts.

Iron Eyes did not mince his words. 'Hell. I like that horse a whole lot more than I like you, Squirrel.'

'How come?'

The bounty hunter snapped his guns shut and then whispered in her face. 'He ain't never shot me.'

Then the bank robbers stopped firing once again. This time it seemed as though the silence lasted for ever.

'They're gonna get on them horses and ride,' Sally said with a knowing nod of her head.

There was no sound coming from beside the livery. Nothing at all. Iron Eyes held on to both his guns and peered over the top of the trough as water splashed in his face. A cold chill ran the length of the bounty hunter's spine. The small female moved across the wet muddy ground and pressed herself up against his side. He did not notice.

'Why'd they quit shooting?' she asked.

'Could be a couple of reasons,' Iron Eyes drawled. He held his smoking guns in his hands and waited for a target. 'Maybe we killed the whole lot of them.'

She looked at his emotionless features. 'Reckon?'

'Nope,' he answered.

'What's the other reason?'

'They rode off,' Iron Eyes suggested.

'I ain't heard no horses riding off,' she said.

'Me neither.' The bounty hunter shrugged. 'They might be out of ammunition.'

'Ya figures that's it, Iron Eyes?'

'Nope.'

'Then what?' Squirrel shouted in his ear. 'Why'd they quit shooting at us?'

Suddenly Iron Eyes's honed hearing heard something he had never heard before. It was a hissing noise and it was drifting on the night air. At first it sounded like an angry sidewinder, then it became obvious to the bounty hunter exactly what it was.

'Hear that, little 'un?'

She screwed up her features and nodded.

'Yep. I hear me something but I sure don't know what it is. It sounds a bit like a herd of hornets. What is it?'

Then the mysterious sound seemed to rise up into the dark brooding sky above them.

Squirrel Sally looked up at the sky and at the fiery object that was coming straight down at them. Sally hit his arm and pointed upward.

'Look,' she screamed. 'What is that?'

Iron Eyes glanced upward and gasped in horror. 'Damn it all.'

'What?'

His unblinking eyes were glued to the foot-long object with its sparking fuse tail. It had been thrown from behind the high stable doors and was now descending towards its target. Then another identical object flew up from the livery. It too had a tail which spat sparks.

The bounty hunter jumped to his feet, grabbed Sally's hair and dragged her up out of the muddy pool. 'C'mon, ya dumb little fool.'

Squirrel Sally Cooke could feel her hair being pulled from her scalp by its roots as the gaunt man hauled her away from the trough and the building. She was sliding on the mud as her small legs failed to keep pace with those of the bounty hunter.

'What's wrong?' she squealed.

'Dynamite,' Iron Eyes shouted.

The fleeing pair had only covered half the width of the street. The safety of the gap between the buildings where they had left the two cowboys' horses was in sight but beyond reach. The first of the sticks of dynamite exploded as it landed near the printer's office. A mere heartbeat later the second stick also erupted with devastating results.

The building took the full force of both blasts. Flames went out in all directions. Planks were turned into matchwood and rose up into the air. The sound of shattering glass resounded as the sheer force of the blast caught both the bounty hunter and the small female.

They were sent head over heels as they were hit by the invisible power of the shock waves which radiated outwards from the destruction. Iron Eyes was thrown like a rag doll up into the air before crashing through a store window.

Squirrel Sally was knocked off her bare feet. Helplessly she rolled over several times until the store's boardwalk steps brutally stopped her progress.

Flames rose a hundred feet into the dark sky. It was as though daylight had suddenly returned to Cooperville in the middle of the night. The red flames illuminated the entire area around what remained of the blazing building.

Sheriff Welch had made slow progress along the length of Main Street to the debris-strewn corner. Small fires were dotted on top of the mud where the tinder-dry wood burned. The two drenched cowboys flanked the sheriff. Both were wondering whether their prized horses were still alive.

As Welch and the cowboys reached the stunned female the charred printer's façade came crashing down and landed directly in front of them.

'Where's our horses, Sheriff?' one of the cowboys asked.

'Hush the hell up, Clevis,' Welch snorted at the irate wrangler. 'This little lady needs our help before we go looking for any damn horseflesh.'

All three men's attention was drawn to the store and its broken window. A stunned Iron Eyes leaned on the window frame as even more blood poured from his already anaemic form. He shook his head and stepped out on to the boardwalk again.

'Ain't there nothing that can kill ya, boy?' Welch asked the blood-soaked figure who cradled his aching skull in his hands.

Iron Eyes looked at the lawman. 'How'd ya know I ain't already dead, old-timer?'

'Dead 'uns don't bleed like that,' the

sheriff snapped.

The sheriff knelt at Squirrel's side.

'She OK?' the bounty hunter asked.

'Out cold,' Welch replied. He turned her over on to her back. Her torn, sodden shirt revealed her well-developed breasts to the onlookers. Both cowboys smiled.

'Damned if it ain't a gal,' one of the cowboys gasped.

'She sure is tough for a gal though,' the other added. 'She stove my ribs in, kicking me off my pinto.'

Iron Eyes stepped to the edge of the boards and looked down at the female. 'She ain't dead, then?'

'Nope. She ain't dead, Iron Eyes,' Welch answered. He got back on to his feet and waved his hands at the pair of cowboys. 'Get here, boys. I want ya to take this little gal to Doc Brody.'

The bounty hunter's spurs rang out as he made his way back to the store wall next to a bright lantern. 'This is the quietest she's ever bin since I first met her. I kinda like the quiet.'

'Where's my horse?' one of the

cowboys piped up.

Iron Eyes stared at the cowboy through the flood of blood which poured from his scalp and then spat. 'I hates cowboys even more than I hates Apaches.'

The cowboy fell silent.

Iron Eyes pulled a twisted cigar out of one of his pockets, placed it between his bleeding lips. He looked at Welch. 'Ya certain she ain't dead, Sheriff?'

'She's alive. Will ya believe me, boy?' Welch looked at the bounty hunter who somehow managed to remain upright despite his horrific injuries. Iron Eyes withdrew a match from his pocket and sparked it with his thumbnail. 'She's just bin knocked out.'

Iron Eyes inhaled the cigar smoke and savoured it as he stared at the blood which continued to drip from the strands of his limp hair.

'I reckon ya ought to go with these boys to see old Doc as well, Iron Eyes,' the law officer suggested.

'Ain't enough time.' Smoke drifted between the sharp teeth of the bounty hunter, who stared at the blazing building and the huge crater beside it. 'I got me important business to finish, Sheriff.'

'Ya bleeding real bad from ya chest and ya head, boy.'

Iron Eyes said nothing. He pulled a lantern off the wall beside his bony shoulder and dragged his long-bladed Bowie knife from the neck of his boot.

The cowboys and the sheriff looked on curiously as the thin skeletal opened the glass window to reveal the naked flame of the lantern. He turned it up until the flame was burning furiously.

'W-what ya figuring on doing, boy?' Welch asked.

'I'm figuring on stopping the bleeding,' Iron Eyes said.

The three men watched as the blade of the knife was placed over the burning wick and held there until it darkened. Then Iron Eyes brought the hot knife-edge to the cut on his chest. The smell of burning flesh chilled the onlookers.

'Holy Moses,' the wettest of the cowboys gulped.

Iron Eyes heated the knife blade up once more.

Sheriff Welch stepped closer to the boardwalk. 'Ya ain't gonna put that red-hot poker on that gash on ya head, are ya?'

Iron Eyes did not respond.

He simply removed the Bowie knife from the flame, raised the blade up and pressed it against the cut on his head. It hissed as the skin melted and the flow of blood stopped.

Without any sign of feeling the pain Iron Eyes hung the lantern back on its hook, then silently walked back to the cowboys, who were standing open-mouthed, watching him. He dipped the blade of the knife into a water trough and then returned it to the neck of his high-sided mule ear boot.

The heat of the fire opposite them drew sweat from the cowboys and the lawman. Only Iron Eyes did not sweat.

The sheriff cleared his throat and waved his arms at the cowboys again before pointing down at the bare-chested female at their feet. 'Pick her up.'

Both cowboys did as they were told and lifted the limp Squirrel Sally off the wet ground. Neither had the nerve to mention anything about their horses to the fearsome figure who sucked silently on his cigar.

Iron Eyes swayed as he stared beyond the burning house to the livery stable.

Welch rested a hand on the muddy sleeve of the bounty hunter's trail coat. 'What ya looking at, boy?'

Smoke trailed from the lips of the tall figure.

'They've gone,' he said.

'The bank robbers?'

Iron Eyes nodded. 'Yep.'

'I'll round up a posse and head on out after them,' Welch said. He followed the long-legged hunter of men to the livery stable. 'Ya tried ya best to stop the critters. Now it's my job to round them up.'

They entered the livery and stopped beside the crumpled body of Stogey Swift, who was still lying behind the door. Then they heard a sound and both went for their guns before recognizing the burly blacksmith who had at last managed to free himself of the ropes which had kept him hogtied for so long.

Slim moved close to the men and rested a hand on the door. 'I sure thought I was a goner, Sheriff.'

'By the looks of all that blood on ya shoulders, them outlaws must have figured they'd done for ya,' Welch said drily.

'Did ya get the rest of them?' Slim asked.

'Nope.' Sheriff Welch sighed. 'But I'm gonna round up a posse at sunup and hunt them down.'

'I'm riding after them alone,' Iron Eyes announced.

'But it's my job,' the sheriff protested.

'Not now. Now it's personal,' the thin man growled.

Slim and the lawman looked at one another as Iron Eyes stared down at the damp ground close to the stable wall.

He nodded and then looked at the blacksmith.

'Did ya get a good look at all the outlaws, Slim?'

'Sure did,' Slim told him. 'One of them only had one leg.'

The bounty hunter wandered out into the street and nodded knowingly to himself. 'Peg Leg Grimes.'

Welch and Slim followed the thin man.

'Peg Leg?' Welch repeated the name. 'Is he wanted dead or alive?'

'He is now,' Iron Eyes boomed.

'What ya mean?'

The bounty hunter sucked the last of the smoke from his cigar and then tossed it away. 'He stole my horse and that means only one thing.'

'What does it mean, boy?'

'What does it mean?' Iron Eyes spat and strolled to where he had secreted the cowboys' horses. 'It means that I'm gonna kill him and the rest of them varmints, old-timer. Nobody steals my horse and lives.'

'What about my posse?'

'I don't need me no stinking posse, Sheriff,' he said over his shoulder. 'I am Iron Eyes. I ride alone.'

Slim and the lawman watched the gruesome figure walk away from the livery stable. Like a phantom he disappeared in the choking smoke of the blazing building as it swept across the muddy street.

Slim looked down at the lawman as the two of them started to walk back to the heart of Cooperville. 'Reckon them bank robbers don't know what they done bit off, Sheriff. That skinny critter ain't gonna quit until either they're all dead or he is.'

Before Jonas Welch could respond both men heard the sound of pounding hoofs somewhere beyond the swirling smoke. Then, like something from their darkest nightmares Iron Eyes cut out from the dense smoke astride one of the cowboys' pinto.

The cadaverous bounty hunter was standing in his stirrups and whipping the shoulders of the powerful cutting horse. The wide-eyed animal was tugging at its reins, trying to escape the relentless thrashing of the long leathers. But there was no escape from the rider who, some believed, was Satan's spawn. A man who could never be killed because he was no longer truly alive.

The horse thundered past the two onlookers. The horseman did not even give them a second glance. They were not what he was after. They were not the wanted men who had nearly killed him and the small Sally Cooke.

Iron Eyes had the scent of his prey in his flared nostrils and he would never quit until he had caught and killed them. Both Slim and Welch stared in disbelief at the sight of the horseman galloping out of town in the direction the four bank robbers had taken only ten minutes earlier. His mane of long black hair bounced on what remained of his long trail coat like the wings of a vulture closing in on something which was already dead but had yet to realize it.

'Nope,' Slim murmured to himself. 'Them outlaws ain't got no idea of what's on their stinking tails, Jonas.'

Welch smiled. 'They'll find out soon enough, Slim.'

12

The smell of neglect filled the interior of Doc Brody's front parlour, which doubled as his office. It was neat and yet dusty the way all unmarried men's residences tend to be. A number of books filled ancient bookcases along the wall and a couch stood in the centre of the room, close to a cluttered desk. It was as if everything had arrived twenty years before and nothing new had been added.

After overseeing the town's primitive firefighters and managing to prevent the fire from spreading from the printer's destroyed office building, Sheriff Welch had eventually made time to have his own injuries looked at by the town's only medical practitioner. The weary lawman tapped on the door and entered with Squirrel Sally's Winchester in his hands. Doc Brody gave a silent nod of recognition to the sheriff and then returned his attention back to his unconscious patient.

Squirrel had a bump on her temple the size of a duck egg and was still oblivious to everything that had occurred since the dynamite blast had sent her crashing head first into the boardwalk steps. Her petite frame barely filled two-thirds of the couch and belied the feisty character the lawman knew her to be.

'Ain't she woke up yet, Doc?'

'Not yet, Jonas.'

Welch noticed that the female had a new shirt covering her modesty. He removed his Stetson and placed it on the top of the desk before moving closer.

'How is she, Doc?' the sheriff asked.

'She'll be OK. I checked her for broken bones but apart from this lump on her head she seems fine.' Brody turned on his chair away from the couch and sighed. 'One of them cowpokes give her the shirt. It's about ten sizes too big but it's in better condition than the other one.'

Welch nodded. 'I got her gun here.'

'That Winchester belongs to her?' Brody lifted his bones off the seat, went gingerly to his desk and picked up a small bottle. He then returned to the comfortable seat and lowered himself down as he unscrewed the stopper.

'Yep. And she knows how to use it,' Welch told him. He looked at the bottle in the doctor's hands. 'What ya got there?'

'Smelling salts,' Brody answered as he carefully moved the bottle under the female's nostrils in a fanning motion. 'Should wake her up unless she's got herself some brain damage.'

The lawman edged closer and watched as Sally's eyelids started to flutter. 'This little critter is the most dangerous gal I ever come across, Doc. A tiger that looks like a kitten.'

Brody paused. 'How'd ya mean?'

Welch showed him the rifle. 'She can shoot up a storm and no mistake with this thing.'

'She's not likely to try and shoot me, is she, Jonas?'

The lawman exhaled thoughtfully. 'I doubt it but ya never can tell with wildcats.'

'Wildcats?' Doc Brody repeated the word and swallowed hard.

'This is the gal who come in on the stagecoach full of dead outlaws with that bounty hunter,' the sheriff explained. 'She has him real scared.'

Doc Brody returned the bottle under her nose. 'I heard folks talking about him. Ain't his name Iron Eyes?'

'Yep. That's his handle.'

Suddenly Squirrel blinked and opened her eyes. It was as if the mere name of the deadly bounty hunter had brought her out of her enforced sleep. Her confused eyes looked at the old doctor and then at the lawman; then she eased herself up off the couch until she was sitting.

'Where is he?' she asked Welch.

'Who?' Welch licked his bleeding lips.

Faster than either man had seen anyone move before she shot up on to her knees, grabbed the sheriff by his double chin and dragged his gun from its holster. She pushed the barrel into his throat and cocked its hammer.

'Don't go messing with me, ya fat old bastard,' she warned. 'Where's Iron Eyes? If he's dead I wanna know.'

'He ain't dead, gal.'

Her eyes hardened as she gritted her teeth. 'Then why ain't he here? Where is the long drink of water?'

'He rode out of town,' Welch squealed.

'When?'

'An hour or so back.'

'He's gone? Damn his hide.' She pushed the gun even harder into his flesh. 'He ain't no good without me to cover his backside. Where'd he go?'

'After the bank robbers,' Welch managed to say as she squeezed his throat even more tightly. 'He was all riled up coz they stole his horse.'

She released her grip, dropped his gun back into its holster and slid to the floor. Both men glanced at one another.

'I could arrest ya for that, Squirrel,' Welch said, backing away and rubbing his throat. 'Ya ain't allowed to strangle law officers.'

Squirrel Sally snatched the rifle from his hands and cocked it. A spent casing flew out of the magazine and bounced off the bookcase. 'I'd sure not recommend ya up and try to arrest me, fat boy. Not unless ya tired of living.'

'Now I see what ya meant, Jonas,' Brody said with a sigh.

'I need me a horse.' She poked the sheriff in the stomach, gave the new shirt a strange look and then tucked it into her threadbare pants. 'A fast horse. The fastest one in town. I gotta catch up with Iron Eyes.'

The lawman kept well away from the small snarling female as she walked towards him with the cocked rifle clutched in her tiny hands.

'But there ain't no horses for sale in town,' Welch informed her. 'The good 'uns were taken by them bank robbers.'

'I still need me a horse,' Squirrel growled. 'The fastest ya damn well got. That pinto I stole will do just fine.'

'Iron Eyes took the pinto,' the sheriff barked.

'He done what?' she yelled.

Welch leaned over and looked hard at her. 'Listen up, Squirrel. There ain't no other fit nags in Cooperville, gal. Savvy?'

Both men could see the fire in her blazing eyes as she managed to contain her fury. She waved a finger at them.

'Reckon I'll have to see about that.' Squirrel Sally tucked the rifle under her armpit, turned the door handle and marched out into the dimly lit street. 'I'll find me something to ride, ya dumb old bastard. Mark my words. I'll find something to get me on Iron Eyes's damn trail.'

Doc Brody put the smelling salts under his own nose, inhaled and then blinked hard. His watery eyes stared sympathetically at his old friend.

'Wildcats ain't got nothing on that little 'un, Jonas.'

Sheriff Welch cautiously looked around the open door frame and then back at the doctor. 'I sure hope she don't go killing nobody, Doc. I'd sure hate to have to try and arrest her.'

Squirrel had only just reached the hotel when a stagecoach rolled round the corner and pulled up outside the stage depot.

She smiled.

'Perfect.'

13

Iron Eyes charged up the dusty rise into the morning light and looked down towards the sparkling river a few hundred yards below. It had been obvious by the trail left for him to follow that none of the bank robbers seemed really to know where they were or where they were going. The injured rider steadied his mount, then spurred it on down towards the small village. The nearer both horse and master got to Red Pepper the more ominous the sight became. Tree-covered mountains lay just beyond the river and the whitewashed adobe buildings, which had once resounded with the voices of those who lived in the small town. As the bounty hunter dragged rein and slowed the pinto the familiar stench of death assailed his nostrils. Suddenly he knew that there was a damn good reason for the silence he faced. The sky was no longer black. There were no more storm clouds battling in the vast heavens. Now the glowing embers of dawn began to usher away the stars and warm the ground.

But with sunup came the truth. The bitter, stomach-churning truth. As the rays of the bright morning sun raced across the ground towards him his eyes absorbed the horror he had ridden into and discovered.

Iron Eyes steadied the pinto beneath him with his strong bony hands as he hovered in his stirrups. He stared out at the scene below him. The horse wanted to turn away from the stench which rose up from the now derelict buildings but Iron Eyes kept jabbing his spurs into its already bleeding flesh. The pinto eventually reached the first of the adobes and was allowed to stop by the unblinking horseman astride it.

The bounty hunter cast his eyes around him. Wherever he looked it was the same vision of murderous death.

As the sun spread out across the wide, shallow river and found even more dead bodies to illuminate, the full horror of what had occurred suddenly dawned on Iron Eyes.

He looked all around him, unable to comprehend why there were so many bodies scattered between the adobe houses. This made no sense to the man who earned his dubious living by killing those the law was too busy to apprehend itself. He killed for a reason but this was different. Totally different.

These lifeless souls had been slaughtered.

Iron Eyes tried to calm the restive horse beneath him. It, like its the rider, was confused.

The thin skeletal horseman had handed out his fair share of death over the years to those wanted dead or alive but this was a massacre.

He dismounted and had to drag the unwilling pinto to a tree and tether its reins firmly. The stench of decomposing bodies was growing riper.

The bounty hunter sucked in his cheeks and tried to remain as cold and calculating as he usually was. But even the hardened soul of the thin man could not simply ignore this. Someone had killed every single person in this small settlement for no good reason. His narrowed eyes studied each of the bodies in turn as he slowly walked between them. The haunting sound of his spurs hung on the morning air. He strode to the very end of the town and began to make his way back. He entered each of the white-washed buildings in turn as he retraced his steps.

He did not count them.

There were too many to count.

Men, women, young and old. All slain without mercy.

Upon reaching the skittish pinto once more he paused and pulled out a broken half-cigar and placed it between his bloodied lips. A match was found and ignited.

Smoke trailed from his mouth.

Not one of them had anything resembling a weapon. He had walked through the whole town in less than two minutes and not seen anything more formidable than a few machetes.

They all lay where they had been shot. His stomach churned in revulsion. Who on earth could have killed so many of these peaceful people he kept asking himself?

What depraved creature took guns to folks who had nothing to defend themselves with?

Iron Eyes sucked in smoke and brooded. His mind raced and searched for the answer. He knew that the leader of the gang was Peg Leg Grimes. That was certain. There were no other wanted bank robbers with only one leg in this part of the West. As the smoke tormented his screwed-up eyes the emaciated man covered in dried blood tried to recall the details he had once read on the Wanted poster with Grimes's image upon it.

'Think, Iron Eyes,' he snarled to

himself as he vainly tried to cast his eyes where there were no bodies. 'Who rides with that one-legged bastard? Grimes would never have done this, but he might have ordered it done.'

As though the details of every Wanted poster he had ever seen were carved into the granite of his memory he began to nod to himself. At last his tired brain started to respond as he shook the weariness from his soul. His fists clenched.

A face filled his thoughts. A face. A name and a price tag.

'Laredo Cole,' Iron Eyes muttered as his teeth gripped the cigar firmly. 'Wanted dead or alive. One thousand dollars.'

It had been a long time since Iron Eyes had last encountered Cole. Four years to be exact. It had been in Yuma. Cole had been young then but was obviously insane to any one who had eyes in their head. Laredo Cole had only survived the meeting with the notorious Iron Eyes because at that time he was not a wanted outlaw.

As more smoke filled his lungs Iron Eyes began to remember that only a year later he had heard that Cole had joined the Grimes gang. It was his speed and accuracy with his guns which had kept him in the gang. Of all those who rode with Grimes it had been Cole who killed for the sheer joy of it. The bounty hunter allowed the smoke to filter through his teeth as his hands pulled his reins free of the tree.

Then suddenly he heard a sound.

A pitiful sound.

Iron Eyes spun on his heels away from the pinto and took a step into the sunlight. His spurs rang out as he tilted his head and listened hard.

Then he heard it again.

He knew exactly what it was making the pathetic noise. His heart pounded inside his chest with a mixture of sadness and revulsion.

Like a hound with the scent of a raccoon in its nostrils the tall man marched between the bodies until he

reached one of the small white adobe
He pulled the cigar from his mouth an
tossed it aside.

Iron Eyes stooped and entered the
dark house which he had looked into
only a few minutes earlier. His eyes
adjusted swiftly to the dim interior of
the house and then he saw what was
making all the noise.

He could hardly swallow. He carefully stepped over the body of a
white-haired female and then rested. A
tiny arm was moving out from the
blanket where the baby's mother had
died beside her most precious posses-
sion. Iron Eyes inhaled deeply and then
knelt down beside the dead female and
the bundle she had tried to protect only
moments before Laredo Cole must
have fanned his gun hammer. There
was blood everywhere. Most of it dry.
Most but not all.

Iron Eyes reached down and managed to free the newly born child from
the blanket and its mother's arms. As
he lifted the infant free his eyes focused

on the savage wound in the tiny baby.

He gasped.

'Damn it all, little 'un. How come ya ain't dead?' he sighed, bringing the dying baby close to his scarred chest. He rose to his full height and walked back out into the sunlight cradling the child as it whimpered.

'Ain't nothing I can do,' he whispered. His lips brushed the top of the infant's tuft of dark hair. 'Nothing but hold ya until . . . '

But there was something the bounty hunter could do. He could remain with the baby until it joined the rest of its kinfolk in a much more peaceful place.

Iron Eyes sat on a barrel and held the dying child. Blood trickled through his fingers and covered his arms but the bounty hunter remained until the whimpering ceased and the last embers of life had drained away from the tiny victim.

Sensing the child was dead, Iron Eyes rose to his feet and stared out across the river. He gritted his teeth. He had

never felt this way before. A fury filled his very soul. A burning fury that was unlike any that he had ever felt before. There was a tempest raging inside Iron Eyes greater than the one which had swept over the plains the night before.

'Ya can ride as fast as ya likes, Laredo,' Iron Eyes screamed at the top of his voice at the unseen outlaws. 'But there ain't no place ya can hide this side of Hell itself. Nobody can hide from Iron Eyes. I'll get ya. Ya all dead. As dead as this little critter.'

This was no longer about the stealing of his prized palomino stallion.

This was now about the lifeless baby in his arms.

The fearsome-looking man looked at the head of the child and pressed his lips against its still sweet-smelling hair. He staggered like a drunkard away from the adobe and stood like a statue in the middle of the countless bodies.

A tear ran from his left eye.

'Sleep, little 'un.'

* * *

Iron Eyes had been correct. They were lost. Peg Leg Grimes and his three cohorts had little idea which trail to take without Stogey Swift to guide them. The trails seemed to split off in at least three separate directions. Stands of trees were everywhere and there was nothing left of the tracks they had left on their journey to Cooperville. The storm had washed the top soil from the steep hillside, leaving nothing recognizable for the desperate eyes of the outlaw leader. Grimes looked all around the forest trying to see if his memory might be jogged by something recognizable. A tree-stump or a giant boulder. Anything which might guide them on the right route.

But unless you were familiar with this strange terrain all the trees appeared identical.

The one-legged outlaw stopped his grey and turned in his saddle to look back at the three other horsemen who were guiding their heavily laden string of horses behind him.

The horses were weighed down under the burden of so much gold coin on their backs and were not making the pace that Grimes knew they would have to make if they were to avoid being caught by anyone daring enough to follow.

Boston Brown was slumped in his saddle a few yards from Grimes. He had not spoken since they had ridden away from the livery stable back at Cooperville. As the morning sun cut across the hillside Grimes suddenly realized that the once unparalleled explosives champion had lost every vestige of colour from his face. He looked like a ghost astride his horse. Only the fact that his eyes were watching the one-legged rider told Grimes that Brown was still alive. Grimes steered his grey with a tug of his reins until he was staring straight into the ashen face.

'Dynamite?' Grimes mumbled.

Brown gave a slight nod. 'Peg Leg.'

'What's wrong?' Grimes queried.

There was no answer, just a wan smile.

Grimes swung his mount around and signalled to Parsons. The youngest of the gang rode up to the side of the troubled Grimes.

'Ya want me, Peg Leg?' Parsons asked.

'Yep.' Grimes snarled and waved at the several trails that led in various directions. 'Do you have any idea which way Stogey brought us, boy?'

'Nope.' Parsons squinted and looked at each of the options in turn. 'Reckon it must be the low trail, though. I sure can't recall us riding high. It was dark as I recall.'

Grimes whistled to Cole. He watched the deadly outlaw spur hard and ride up the slope towards them.

'What ya want, Peg Leg?' Cole asked, keeping both eyes on the string of horses just below them.

'Which of these damn trails do we take, Laredo?' Grimes asked, looking down into the valley below them where the wide river sparkled in the morning sun. 'Which one do ya figure Stogey brung us along?'

Cole pushed his hat back and pondered. 'I recall us cutting around a real big rock near a pool.'

'I recall that as well.' Parsons nodded.

'Yeah, but where the hell is that rock and that pool, boys?' Grimes was getting anxious. He knew that it would not be long before someone set out from Cooperville in pursuit of their hides and the gold they had stolen. 'I figure we oughta take the middle trail.'

The attention of all three outlaws was drawn to Brown, who was making a strange choking noise. As they watched he fell from his saddle on to the unforgiving soil. Brown stared with dead eyes up at the sky as Parsons leapt to the ground and rushed to his motionless form.

'How is he?' Grimes asked.

Parsons ripped Brown's shirt open and placed an ear on his pale chest. A few seconds later he straightened up and shook his head. 'Dead,' he gasped.

191

'Dynamite's dead.'

For a few moments Grimes said nothing. Then he snapped his fingers and silently indicated to Parsons to get back on his horse.

The young outlaw mounted and stared down at the lifeless Brown in total disbelief. 'How come he just up and died?'

'Let that be a warning to ya, Winston. Too many Mexican whores done for him,' Cole snarled. 'He must have been riddled with pox from all them whores.'

Grimes raised a hand to his eyes and shielded the sun from his face. He stared down at the town they had destroyed, far below them, then he noticed something amid all the carnage.

'Hey, boys,' he said. His finger pointed to the heart of Red Pepper. 'Am I seeing things or is that someone walking around down there?'

Cole turned his horse and squinted hard to where Grimes was indicating. 'Ain't no posse but I reckon ya might be right, Peg Leg. Looks like there's someone down there.'

Grimes nodded. 'I thought so. That means that they've made ground up on us. Where there's one there'll be more coming pretty soon.'

'It's this damn trail, Peg Leg,' Cole ranted. 'It's too damn steep for these horses to carry the gold over. These nags will never get over this damn mountain before someone gets us in range of their hogleg.'

Parsons cleared his throat. 'What about Dynamite?'

Grimes ignored the question and turned his horse to face the string of horses lined up on the trail. 'We're heading back down this trail.'

Cole looked at Grimes long and hard. 'Going back down? Are ya serious?'

'Dead serious.' Grimes nodded. 'Ya right, Laredo. We'll get picked off by anyone with a half-decent rifle before we even haul these nags another half-mile. The only chance we got is to head on back down and kill whoever is on our trail.'

'What then?' Cole asked.

'We head south with the gold. South into Mexico.'

'Into Mexico?' Cole was horrified.

'Yep. It's flat all the way.' Grimes rode over to the string of horses. He grabbed the reins of the lead horse and turned the animal. 'C'mon.'

'What about Dynamite, Peg Leg?' Parson repeated.

'To hell with him, Winston,' Grimes shouted over his shoulder, 'Now, c'mon! We gotta stop that *hombre* down there and make it plain to any posse that shows up that it don't pay to follow us. Then we head south.'

'I don't cotton to riding into Mexico,' Cole yelled out as he rode next to his leader.

'Look on the bright side, Laredo.' Grimes spat. 'At least you'll have plenty of folks to shoot and kill down there.'

The three outlaws began to lead the string of horses back down to the range.

There was no posse to face.

Only one man stood between them and freedom.

Iron Eyes.

It had not taken long for Iron Eyes to bury the small child in the soft ground. His hands had scooped out enough of the white sand to ensure that no wild animal would catch her scent and dig her up again. The thin man patted the ground down and then stood and looked around at all the other bodies. In all his days he had never seen any-thing so totally pointless and it incensed him almost as much as discovering the dying baby in its mother's arms.

Iron Eyes looked down at the unmarked grave. 'I'll come back and bury ya ma next to ya, little 'un,' he vowed. 'I got me some scores to settle first.'

He marched to the pinto, dragged his reins free and threw himself up into the saddle. He gathered the leathers together, swung the horse around and jabbed his spurs into its flanks.

The horse cantered across the ground, picking its way between the bodies, until it reached the river. The horseman eased back on his reins and then studied the ground. There were hoof-tracks leading straight into the fast-flowing water. A lot of hoof tracks, and one set of them belonged to his palomino stallion.

'Ya better not let me down, horse.' Iron Eyes eased his grip on the reins and allowed the animal to drop its head and drink from the cold clear water. 'Four of them laden down with bags of gold. Heavy gold. By my figuring I'll catch up with them before noon. Then I'll kill 'em all.'

Iron Eyes pushed the last of his cigars into his mouth and scratched a match with his thumbnail. The flame was captured between his hands, the cigar lit, and the smoke was inhaled, long and deep. Iron Eyes knew that the four men ahead of him were little different from all those he had hunted over the years. The only exception was Laredo Cole.

Back in Yuma Iron Eyes had sensed that the young gunslinger had a streak of insanity running through him. For some reason known only to Cole himself he loathed anyone who appeared remotely Mexican. It made no sense to the bounty hunter to waste energy hating anyone, apart from those who tried to kill him.

The smell of death was growing stronger behind his broad shoulders. The sun was becoming warmer. The bounty hunter cast his eyes over his shoulder at the scene of carnage and knew that this was Cole's handiwork.

Iron Eyes nodded knowingly to himself and held the reins in his hands. Only Cole could hate an entire village of helpless people so badly that he had to destroy them. Being an expert tracker, Iron Eyes had studied the boot-impressions in the sand around the bodies. This was the work of just one man. He had moved from one unarmed person to the next, gleefully fanning his gun hammers.

'Cole.' The name drifted on the smoke which filtered through Iron Eyes's thin lips. 'Ya gonna pay for this, boy. Pay high.'

Iron Eyes pulled the head of the pinto up and steadied the animal by balancing in the stirrups. He thought about Cole for a few moments.

Cole was a mad dog.

Iron Eyes knew he had to kill him.

Kill him before the locobean found another village peopled by those whose appearance or accents upset him and forced him into repeating this carnage.

The bounty hunter checked his deep pockets for bullets and came up shy of the amount he needed for his pair of matched Navy Colts. One by one he slid the last .36s into the chambers of his guns.

He only had eight bullets left.

His eyes narrowed as vainly he searched the other side of the river for his prey. The rest of his ammunition was in one of the satchels of his bags and they were laced to the cantle of his fancy Mexican saddle somewhere out there. Somewhere out there on the back of his palomino stallion.

Iron Eyes dragged the cowboy's rifle from its scabbard under the fender of his right leg and jerked its hand guard. He looked into the magazine and pulled the brass lever back.

'Only two bullets and a mess of cob-webs,' he complained as he returned the long-barrelled weapon to the scabbard. 'Damn it all. Cowboys never keep their damn weapons loaded. I hates cowboys almost as much as I hates Apaches. Ain't never no profit in stealing a cow-boy's horse.'

The skeletal rider spurred his mount onward.

Plumes of ice-cold water rose all around them as the pinto plunged across the river.

The ground on the opposite bank was soft and still trying to absorb the tempestuous downpour which had nearly drowned him and Squirrel when they were shooting it out with Grimes and his gang back at Cooperville.

The bounty hunter kept on relent-lessly driving his spurs into the pinto, forcing it to find a pace which did not suit a cutting horse. The horse had covered a good quarter-mile when Iron Eyes felt the heat of a bullet passing within inches of his head. Then the sound caught up with the bullet and echoed around the flat terrain.

Not waiting either to feel or hear a second shot, Iron Eyes drew rein and leapt from the saddle. As he hit the ground the pinto shied, tore the reins from the bounty hunter's hand and bolted off in the opposite direction.

Iron Eyes crouched and watched the horse galloping away. He gritted his teeth. 'There goes the rifle. Damn it all.'

Then another shot rang out. The soft ground beside him was kicked up and mud splattered all over him. Iron Eyes dragged both his guns from his pants belt and dropped on to his belly.

He squinted into the sun, then he saw them.

Another shot hissed as it caught the shoulder padding of his trail coat and almost flipped him over.

'That was too close,' Iron Eyes growled like a cornered mountain lion. He managed to roll a few feet from where he had landed.

The riders had him in their sights.

All three were closing in on him fast and furiously. Suddenly all of their guns began to spew venomous lead at him. The ground started to erupt all around his outstretched form. Iron Eyes wanted to return fire but knew that he only had eight bullets in his two Navy Colts.

He rolled over and over until he was in long reeds. He paused and listened as more and more bullets were fired. They wanted him as badly as he wanted them, he thought.

Scrambling to his knees Iron Eyes saw them. They were now less than 200 yards from him. As he raised his weapons he saw Cole and recognized him.

'Cole.' He spat.

The three outlaws still had the rest of the horses in tow as Parsons spotted the gaunt emaciated figure to their left. He dragged his reins hard and started to ride at the bounty hunter. With each stride of his mount he fired his guns in turn.

Bullets passed all around the bounty

hunter as he defiantly stood upright and raised one of his guns.

Iron Eyes fired.

His bullet hit the horseman dead centre.

Parsons seemed to float off the back of his horse before he crashed to the ground behind his mount's hoofs. Iron Eyes did not waste time wondering if his aim had been true. He had seen the bullet hit the youngster's chest. No heart was strong enough to withstand a bullet.

Another volley of shots rang out across the range. Iron Eyes felt the tails of his long coat being ripped apart as both Grimes's and Cole's bullets tore through its frail fabric.

Iron Eyes turned and raised both his guns.

Cole hauled his leathers to his chest and jumped down from his saddle. Grimes kept on coming. The bounty hunter snarled as he watched Cole vanish into the long swaying grass and reeds a hundred yards from him. He jumped to one side as the outlaw's horse thundered past him.

Then he saw Grimes whipping his horse's shoulders with the tails of his reins. The outlaw leader was closing in on the bounty hunter far faster than Iron Eyes had imagined possible.

Iron Eyes squeezed both triggers.

The horse buckled and dropped head first into the ground, sending its one-legged master hurtling over its neck. Grimes was a lot tougher than he looked. The outlaw hit the soft ground and somersaulted. Grimes struggled to stand, but his wooden stump sank into the soft ground. Furiously he blasted his gun at the snarling Iron Eyes. The white-hot taper cut through the morning air and carved a furrow across the bounty hunter's cheek. Iron Eyes staggered backwards a few steps before he managed to raise his guns again.

Blood flowed freely from a savage gash across Iron Eyes's already mutilated face. A cruel smile etched its way through the blood.

'Close, but no cigar, Peg Leg,' Iron

Eyes hissed before firing his guns again. He watched Grimes's hefty bulk lift off the ground and fly backwards.

Only the wooden leg remained in the spot where the outlaw had been standing a mere heartbeat earlier.

There was no time to gloat. As smoke billowed from the barrels of the Navy Colts the injured bounty hunter crouched once more and tried to work out where Cole was. He cocked both hammers again and began to walk to where the outlaw had vanished.

Four steps later Laredo Cole leapt up to the right of Iron Eyes and blasted both his guns again.

Rods of hot lead homed in on their target. Iron Eyes swung round on one leg and saw his attacker. Once again the long tails of his trail coat were almost torn from him as the bullets ripped into them. Another two shots followed from Cole's smoking barrels.

Iron Eyes had lost count of how many bullets he had already fired or how many he still had left in his guns, but it did not matter to him. Something deep inside him knew that he would not die until Laredo Cole had been eliminated.

'Laredo Cole,' the bounty hunter blazed across the distance between them. 'Was it you who killed all them pitiful folks down yonder, boy?'

Stunned, Cole stared at the horrific sight. He was confused by the sight of the man drenched in his own blood coming at him with his guns levelled. Cole remembered seeing this creature years before.

'Iron Eyes?' he gasped. The guns in his hands began to shake as fear swept through every sinew in his body.

'Well? Did ya?' Iron Eyes yelled. He got closer and closer to the man he wanted to kill more than any other man he had ever encountered. 'Did ya kill all them harmless critters over there? Did ya?'

'What if I did?' Cole croaked, fear gripping his throat like a hangman's rope. 'Ya gonna do anything about it?'

'Damn right.' Iron Eyes squeezed

back on his triggers. His guns blasted the last of his bullets into the vicious killer. The outlaw seemed to grow a few inches as both bullets hit him in the guts. Blood began to pour from the two neat holes in his shirt before he fell on his knees. Then more blood trailed from his mouth but he was not dead and he still held on to his guns with shaking hands.

'Reckon ya out of bullets, Iron Eyes,' Laredo Cole sneered, and raised both his weapons to aim at the bounty hunter. 'Meet ya in Hell.'

Iron Eyes felt his fingers pulling on empty chambers. 'Ya could be right, boy.'

Then suddenly a rifle shot rang out. A bullet hit the kneeling outlaw in the side of his head. Gore exploded from Cole's skull before he hit the ground. With the sound of the shot still echoing in his ears Iron Eyes turned and saw the stagecoach at the river's edge with the familiar female standing on its roof.

Squirrel Sally waved her Winchester at him.

'Did I just save ya life again there, Iron Eyes?' she called out. She expelled the hot casing from her trusty rifle. 'Did I, ya ornery bastard?'

Iron Eyes pushed both his guns down into his empty trail coat pockets and turned. He saw his palomino stallion tethered to all the other horses. He whistled and the powerful horse started towards him with all the other animals in tow. Iron Eyes returned his attention to the small female standing on top of the stagecoach.

'Got any whiskey, Squirrel?'

She raised a bottle of amber liquor. 'Sure have. Stole me a whole box of cigars as well.'

Iron Eyes grabbed the saddle horn of his palomino, dragged himself up on to the fancy saddle and spurred. He slowed when he reached the stagecoach, untied the other horses and tossed the reins to Squirrel.

'Tie this string of horses to the tail-gate, gal.'

She looked at him curiously. 'Don't

ya want a drink?'

Iron Eyes aimed his horse at Red
Pepper. 'Got me a chore to do first,
little 'un.'

Squirrel Sally placed the whiskey bottle
down on the roof of the coach and
watched him spur and steer the powerful stallion across the river towards the
little town.

Finale

The jailhouse cell was filled with the bags of gold coins that had been dragged from the stagecoach. Sheriff Welch dusted himself off with his hands and looked at the tall injured man who was resting a bony hand on the bars.

'How come ya didn't bring the bodies of them bank robbers back for the bounty, boy?' Welch asked the man, who was chewing a fresh cigar.

'Didn't want to dirty my hands, Sheriff,' Iron Eyes said. He struck a match and touched the tip of the cigar. 'Reckon the buzzards can have them.'

Both men watched as Squirrel Sally hauled the last of the hefty bags across the office floor and into the cell.

'That the last of them, Squirrel?' the bounty hunter asked.

'Yep.' She nodded as she pushed the bag up against the others. 'Must be a fortune in these bags and no mistake.'

Iron Eyes slammed the barred door shut and turned the key in its lock. He tossed the key into Welch's hands and strode out to the boardwalk with the lawman on his tail.

'What ya lock me in here for, ya pitiful skunk?' Squirrel called out as Iron Eyes closed the office door. 'I saved ya damn life again and ya locks me up?'

'Squirrel got herself a point there,' Welch said as he watched the thin man with the crude stitches in his cheek step into his stirrup and mount the palomino in one easy action. 'What ya go locking her up in there for?'

'To try and get away from her.' Iron Eyes sighed. 'She kinda scares me, Sheriff.'

The shouting from inside the sheriff's office grew louder but both men tried to ignore it.

'I'd have a mountain lion caged in there rather than her, boy,' the lawman admitted. 'That gal is tougher than a barrel of nails.'

Iron Eyes gathered up his reins. 'Hold on to her for a couple of days, Sheriff. Give me time to get away.'

'Ya going?' Welch stared hard at the bounty hunter who drew unhurriedly on his cigar. 'What about all the reward money ya owed?'

'Give it all to her, Sheriff.' Iron Eyes glanced down at the friendly face. 'Maybe she'll find someone else to bother once she got some money.'

The sheriff was about to speak again when both men heard the deafening rifle shot inside the office. Welch blinked hard and looked up at the bounty hunter. 'Damn it all, boy. She must have her Winchester in the cell. She's shooting the damn lock off my cell door.'

'Reckon it's time for me to hightail it. *Adios*.' Iron Eyes tossed his cigar away, then spurred hard. The frightened sheriff buried his face in the palms of his hands as the powerful stallion thundered along Main Street. The horseman turned his head and heard the rifle being fired over and over again. The bounty hunter knew it would not take Squirrel very long to escape and be on his trail again.

Iron Eyes stood in his stirrups and laughed.

We do hope that you have enjoyed reading this large print book.

Did you know that all of our titles are available for purchase?

We publish a wide range of high quality large print books including:
Romances, Mysteries, Classics
General Fiction
Non Fiction and Westerns

Special interest titles available in large print are:
The Little Oxford Dictionary
Music Book, Song Book
Hymn Book, Service Book

Also available from us courtesy of Oxford University Press:
Young Readers' Dictionary
(large print edition)
Young Readers' Thesaurus
(large print edition)

For further information or a free brochure, please contact us at:
Ulverscroft Large Print Books Ltd.,
The Green, Bradgate Road, Anstey,
Leicester, LE7 7FU, England.
Tel: (00 44) **0116 236 4325**
Fax: (00 44) **0116 234 0205**

Other titles in the
Linford Western Library:

THE VINEGAR PEAK WARS

Hugh Martin

Saddle tramps Cephas Dannehar and Slim Oskin, drifting through the Vinegar Peak country of Arizona Territory, help an old colleague out of trouble, and in doing so get themselves on the wrong side of scheming Nate Sturgis, the self-styled boss of Vinegar Peak. In a lead-peppered struggle between their horse-ranching friends and Sturgis's toughs, bullets are soon flying and fires of destruction lit — all part of the growing pains of a raw western territory shaping its post-Civil War destiny . . .

THE SEARCH FOR THE LONE STAR

I. J. Parnham

It has long been rumoured that the fabulous diamond known as the Lone Star is buried somewhere near the town of Diamond Springs. Many men have died trying to claim it, but when Diamond Springs becomes a ghost town, the men who go there have different aims. Tex Callahan has been paid to complete a mission; Rafferty Horn wants to right a past mistake; George Milligan thinks he knows what has happened to the diamond; and Elias Sutherland wants revenge . . .

LAST MAN IN LAZARUS

Bil Shields

When a town marshal is murdered by five escaping prisoners and his new bride is abducted, the killers think they have avoided the justice they deserve. But the dead man's older brother is Nathan Holly, a feared and relentless US marshal who is more than happy to take up the pursuit. Holly rides north with a Paiute tracker, Tukwa — a man conducting his own quest for vengeance. Both will end their search amidst the winter snows of a mining town called Lazarus . . .